SPIRIT OF A HUNDRED THOUSAND DEAD ANIMALS

# SPIRIT OF
# A HUNDRED THOUSAND
# DEAD ANIMALS

Jim Nason

EDITIONS

Cover design by Doowah Design.
Cover image: Anatomical engraving of a horse, from Wellcome Images, a website operated by Wellcome Trust, a global charitable foundation based in the United Kingdom.
Photo of Jim Nason by Don Smith.

This book was printed on Ancient Forest Friendly paper.
Printed and bound in Canada by Hignell Book Printing Inc.

Acknowledgements

We acknowledge the support of the Canada Council for the Arts and the Manitoba Arts Council for our publishing program.

Songs referred to in the text: "Good morning Heartache," Billie Holiday, 1946: written by Irene Higginbotham, Ervin Drake and Dan Fisher; "Strange Fruit," Billie Holiday, 1939: written by Abel Meeropol; "Back in Black," AC/DC, 1980.

Excerpt from "Wild Geese" by Mary Oliver, 1986 Atlantic Monthly Press, New York, NY.

Library and Archives Canada Cataloguing in Publication

Nason, Jim, 1957–, author
      Spirit of a hundred thousand dead animals / Jim Nason.

Issued in print and electronic formats.
ISBN 978-1-77324-021-3 (softcover).
--ISBN 978-1-77324-022-0 (EPUB)

      I. Title.

PS8577.A74S65 2017          C813'.54          C2017-904688-8
                                                                  C2017-904689-6

Signature Editions
P.O. Box 206, RPO Corydon, Winnipeg, Manitoba, R3M 3S7
www.signature-editions.com

*For Joyce Shepard*

*You do not have to be good.*
*You do not have to walk on your knees*
*for a hundred miles through the desert, repenting.*
*You only have to let the soft animal of your body*
*love what it loves.*

from "Wild Geese"
Mary Oliver

# PART I

# KINCARDINE, ONTARIO, 2011

You can die from it. You can crawl face down through the mud, be swallowed by it, if you want, by regret, the gluttonous snake, its jaw clamped on your shivering body, five dirty fingers on each of your hands, ten toes on your blistered feet. You can be pulled through its unhinged mouth.

Skye shakes the image of her son-in-law and the snake from her head, looks at her bloodshot eyes and wrinkled face in the bathroom mirror; so many years since Magnus disappeared. Too many years brushing her hair in the early morning light of the bathroom window, half expecting him to stagger through the front door — hoping he will return, praying he won't. *I'm back for my boy!* he'll announce, probably slurring his words. *I went off the rails for a while, but I'm back for little Duncan.*

"He's not so *little* now, Magnus Johnson," she says in the direction of the front door. "He has the Vannan height and hefty bones, his mother's fair hair and your devilish brown eyes. He's grown up and gone home to Scotland without me."

Skye scrubs her hands and face with the lavender soap that Duncan bought her before he left and dries off with the musty-smelling towel that she probably should have changed a week ago. She inhales, takes another look at her wrinkled face in the mirror, exhales and drops the towel onto the floor. It's been a hot summer and today is no exception. The humidity is oppressive and the pain in her chest has worsened. Silver hair and a bent-over frame, she won't be long for this world. She knows too much about the lifespan of living creatures to pretend otherwise. She places the hairbrush on

the back of the bathroom sink and turns away. Even after she and
Rory married she could still hear her mother's voice — *too tall for a
girl, shoulders too wide for a wedding gown. Skye Vannan, you have the
square frame of a man and jaw of a horse; your looks must come from
your father's side of the family.*

Skye grips her walker tightly and leans forward, shifting her
weight from side to side as she pushes along the dark hallway past
Rocky's broken-down straw basket. "Rocky," she calls, but he does
not come. "Come, Rocky — let me tell you about the mist that
cloaks Edinburgh and the sea creatures that live in Loch Dunvegan."

She shuffles past dustballs like little grey kittens along the
floorboards, into the kitchen with its faded yellow walls and window
looking out over the garden. She parks her walker next to the stove
where the grey squirrel came down from the attic and scampered
into her kitchen through a gap in the wall. Not today. She can't
spend another minute thinking about harm she has caused. There's
no chance of returning to Scotland now, no possibility of correcting
what went wrong; it's time to forget the misdeeds of the past.

Skye had opened her eyes to a nauseating headache. It was
difficult to breathe and she felt weak, but it never occurred to her to
stay in bed. Skye Rayburn didn't survive two wars and the death of her
husband and only daughter to wallow in self-pity. She should drink
a glass of cold water, find the bottle of aspirin. She's not so worried
about dying, she only wishes that Duncan were here to reassure her
in his calm, soothing voice: *It's all right, Grandma Skye,* he'd say. *You're
going to live to be a hundred and fifty.* But she will never see him again;
she can feel it in her bones. The pain in her side is from an old, weak
heart, but it's also about her grandson — he's pulling away, "leaving
the nest," as her mother said to her that morning more than sixty-five
years ago when she and Rory boarded the ship in Leith.

Skye looks at the month of August stuck on the refrigerator with
magnets. She holds a pencil over August 22. Is it really the 22nd? If
so, he will be returning to Kincardine tomorrow.

*I'll be back in a fortnight,* Duncan had teased her as he packed
his suitcase.

She shuffles over to the kitchen table and pulls out her journal from the end drawer: *Life Lessons for Duncan*; there are things that need to be discussed with him right away.

She pushes back to the refrigerator and counts the X's on the calendar — there are fifteen, and Duncan is supposed to be away only two weeks. "Don't start second-guessing yourself, Skye Rayburn," she says out loud. "That's how old people go crazy. Of course he's back tomorrow."

The doctor wouldn't allow her to fly. He started with a lecture about her going into the city alone in search of Magnus. "Dangerous and ridiculous. You could have been killed," Doctor Helliwell said.

"That trip into the city was a year ago," she told him. "Before I became dependent on this cursed walker. Besides, that boy still needs a father."

"Magnus Johnson knows where Kincardine is, Skye. He doesn't need you to drag him back here."

"Sometimes people do things they regret and just don't know how to turn themselves around," she said, looking down at her feet dangling off the examination table.

"Let's get back to this trip to Scotland. Sorry, Skye," he said, removing his cold stethoscope from her chest. "I've been encouraging you to do this for years, and now that it's impossible, you decide to fly home. Not with my blessing," he said. "They'll be sending you back to Kincardine in a pine box."

"Who says I'm coming back?" she said, struggling with the buttons of her blouse. "They can keep my ashes in Scotland."

"I don't think that would sit too well with the people of this town or Duncan," he said.

"The people in this town will not be sentimental about seeing my remains, and Duncan's a grown man now. Besides, he'll be right by my side."

"That's a lot to ask of him, Skye, when he's setting off on his own path."

She wanted Duncan to go to Edinburgh and she wanted to share that moment with him, that's all. She wasn't being selfish.

She was simply trying to address this longing, the nagging need to see Scotland one last time. Then again, Doctor Helliwell was right. There was pain in her chest — a definite, insistent tug beneath her ribs that sometimes took her breath away.

•

She needs to sit, but first she picks the Edinburgh Festival programme off the counter next to the stove. There's an x-ray image of an animal on the cover, a foetal foal. It's both bothersome and intriguing. The Royal Dick Veterinary School was transformed into a venue for the Festival and Duncan has been invited to show his drawings there — dear Lord. Very clever of those Scots to combine science with art by using an image that echoes back to the Royal Dick while bringing the college into something otherworldly for the young people. She flips through the pages and finds Duncan's photo. He's handsome, with sandy hair, bright brown eyes and his grandfather Rory's easy-going manner. Above his picture, his drawing of her beloved dog, Rocky, and the caption for his exhibition of charcoal drawings: *I Was Raised by a Pack of Wolves*. Skye sets the booklet down on the stove. She'd asked where he got such an odd title but he never gave her a clear answer. *I don't know*, he said. *It just came.* Duncan had always held a special relationship with animals; she shouldn't have been surprised. *Kitty cat*, he said when he was just a toddler. *Kitty cat*, he repeated, pointing to her wind-blown hair.

She turns and sits, rests her head on the kitchen table and closes her eyes, thinks back to the day she and Moira brought Duncan home from Kincardine Hospital. How long ago was that now? Of course, he will be twenty-nine on August 27th, and she'll be ninety-one in two weeks. There's nothing wrong with her memory.

On September 2, 1920, at 8:00 a.m., her parents had just arrived for a tour of Dunvegan Castle. They'd been invited by Lord Hill to discuss the issue of managing the countryside crofts. The sheep farmers weren't doing so well and the Vannans, after all, were the largest purchasers of wool in the country. As Skye's mother stood admiring the legendary Fairy Flag with its alleged mystical powers, she felt her water break. There would be no talk of sheep or wool, no time to call for a midwife or doctor. Skye was born right there on the dusty floor of the castle while her mother clutched the tattered, gold banner and cursed her husband for dragging her across the country on such horrendous roads. *Hold fast, darling!* he pleaded. *Hold fast.*

Skye was born into a deep respect for fate and how it weaves itself through landscape and time — her father, holding her up to a window that looked out over Loch Dunvegan, had insisted that a beautiful girl with eyes as blue as hers, born on the Isle with its grassy knolls and wispy clouds, simply had to be called Skye. Her mother must have agreed with the name, but Skye had heard her use it only when she was angry. Otherwise, she would call her *Missy*, or *Child*, but mostly, her mother referred to her as plain old capital Y, *You*.

# EDINBURGH, SCOTLAND, 1938

"You want to become what?" her mother asked.

"A veterinarian."

"There's no polite way of saying this, child, so I'm just going to say it — you have completely lost your young mind."

Skye had thought long and hard about a profession. Scotland was facing a war, and she had to be practical. Besides, she loved animals. From the time she was a child, she considered it her mission to feed the baby bird that had fallen from its nest or to bathe a girth sore on an over-ridden horse. She loved cats and dogs and she wasn't afraid of getting manure on her shoes in the cowshed. She also knew that there was no reasoning with her mother once she'd made up her mind.

"I've talked to Father," Skye said. "And he says I'll be good with animals."

"Your father has no idea when it comes to girls." Her mother folded her arms and dropped back into her favourite chair near the parlour window. "Sit down." She motioned to Skye, but Skye remained standing.

"He says he will pay for my first year at the Royal Dick, and if I don't excel, he will cut off my tuition."

"There's more at stake here than education, Missy. If you head in this direction, not only will you be gangly and awkward, you'll end up dressed and reeking like an 'untouchable' and become as eccentric as your father praying to his shrine of Ganesha each and every time life throws a difficult decision his way."

"From my childhood memory of elephants, Mother, they are pleasant, kind-hearted animals, utterly worthy of worship."

"Don't go mocking me, Skye Vannan," her mother said. "You may think your father holds the purse strings in this family — well, you are terribly wrong about that assumption."

•

Vannan Wool and Manufacturing had its humble beginnings in India. Skye had very little memory of the country, but her mother constantly reminded her of the beautiful silks and detailed cotton fabrics that they'd purchased for their fledgling business. She also warned Skye about their *voodoo religion, the worshipping of cows and elephants*, and how they *cast off the untouchables to the streets of Calcutta*.

Skye had to agree with her mother that her body lacked the curves and grace of other girls her age, and she wasn't interested in the polite conversation that was supposed to attract well-bred boys. *Be attentive,* her mother would say. *Listen and smile when they look like they need some encouragement. Remember the three Ms: money, manners and marriage.* Skye didn't know which way to turn. Maybe her mother was right? Perhaps she should compose herself, be more graceful in the world. But she couldn't imagine that life. Every time she tried to picture herself sitting poised and attentive while her imaginary husband spewed on about his business, she would fall into a fit of despair. Crying wasn't usually effective with her mother, but this time, her mother came around once the tears started flowing.

"Well, all right," she said. "We will give it one year. But mark my words, you will regret this day, and when you're an old spinster living alone, I will not be there to pick you up the way I always have."

Skye hugged her mother and her mother almost hugged her as well — she'd opened her arms and Skye stepped forward; but it seemed she just she couldn't bring herself to embrace her daughter.

"Leave that on the table," she nodded at the application for the Royal Dick Veterinary College that Skye had been clutching.

"Certainly, Mother," Skye said, attempting to flatten out the creases.

"And for the love of Jesus, please brush your hair and put on a proper skirt... We are having guests for dinner. Government officials. There's a war on the horizon, child."

BEAVER

| Species | Castor Canadensis |
|---|---|
| Phylum | Chordata |
| Order | Rodentia |
| Family | Castoridae |
| Description | Largest rodent in North America and the third largest rodent in the world; loves to eat water lilies. |
| Attributes | Skilled tree-cutter and dam-builder; fur is ideal for fashionable hats. |

Life Lesson for Duncan
Build a lodge that's resistant to trespassers.

# EDINBURGH, 1945

"The war's over," Rory said, mustering up the courage to talk to her, "but I wish I had a hand grenade to set under the tram to hurry it along."

Initially, Skye ignored him, but it was dark and rainy and having a soldier next to her was somewhat reassuring. "You have a funny accent," she said.

"Me?" he said. "You're the one with a Scottish accent."

"And where do you think you are?" she'd asked. "I would argue that my accent is perfectly normal in these parts."

At last the tram arrived, only it was too crowded for them to squeeze onto.

"Here," he said, holding the umbrella over Skye. "The rain doesn't bother me at all. We went for days being wet during battle."

Skye looked at the crest on his uniform as he held the umbrella over her dripping head.

"You're from Canada," she said, as they started to walk.

"Yes, I am," he said, stepping a few inches closer to her under the umbrella. "A town called Kincardine."

"Oh. They speak English there then?"

"We try," he laughed. "Kincardine is in a province called Ontario. I'm just a simple farm boy."

He had no idea where they were going; Rory just kept walking, holding the umbrella over her head.

"You have cows and horses?"

"I help my dad run a dairy farm."

"I love animals," she said. "I just graduated from the Royal Dick."

Rory tripped on the cobblestone. He suddenly seemed unable to find the earth beneath his feet.

"It's a veterinary college," she added.

An educated woman, she'd never see him again. Smart girls always ran the other way.

"I don't plan on staying on the farm. I want to build things from wood," he said, holding his arm up, making a muscle. "I'm a carpenter."

"Canada must have plenty of trees for lumber," she said.

"More than you can possibly imagine. And lakes. We live by the biggest lake you've ever seen."

"Really?"

"Huron," he said, trying to keep up with her pace. "You have long legs."

*Walk like a lady. You're gangly as a giraffe. No wonder you're still not married at twenty-five.*

"The rain seems to have stopped," she said, after a few minutes of walking at a slower pace.

"You're right, I guess, but night-time in Edinburgh is no place for a pretty girl to be walking alone."

Rory knew that it hadn't come out right. He knew that he didn't have the charm to pull off flirtations or even a sincere compliment, but he knew that he would never see her again if he didn't say something. "I would be happy to escort you home," he said as they turned off Hogue Park Terrace.

"We're here," she said, stopping abruptly. "And no," she continued, "in answer to your question."

"But I didn't ask you anything yet."

"I've heard," she said. "Soldiers get…lonely."

"I would never do anything to break your trust," he said, and meant it. "I would be honoured to buy you a tea," he said. And noticing that she didn't reject him immediately, added: "I could tell you about the animals in Canada."

"Well," she said, looking down at her hands. "I am interested in the beaver."

"Really?"

"I know this is horrible," she said. "But I've always wanted one of those beaver hats that the women in the New York magazines wear."

*I met a girl,* he wrote his parents. *I survived the war and I met a girl. She's tall with beautiful dark hair and she loves animals. She's smart too — a veterinarian. She'll love the farm. I know it. And I told her that Kincardine has enough pastures for all the cows and pigs and horses she could ever imagine. I told her there was plenty of work to do with animals in Canada and that the University of Toronto could be a place for her to study more if she had to, and I told her about Cornell in New York. And I tried to kiss her at her door and she slapped me. No disrespect, Mom, the war's over and I just wanted to kiss someone (other than the other soldiers on V-Day). I'm the luckiest guy this side of the ocean. Maybe she likes me too.*

*How are things on the farm? Is there lots of milk from the cows now that the worry of the war is over? Is there snow in Canada? It's cold here, and rainy; but beautiful, Mom. The ocean is mighty and the cliffs around Edinburgh are green and give a guy the best view you could ever imagine. We went to a place called Arthur's Seat and were sitting on the cliff and this stray dog came limping along and growling. She knew right what to do and wasn't afraid. Never trust a growling injured dog, I told her, but she called it over and the dog came whimpering to her side. She pulled something out of its paw and it growled just as she yanked it and she didn't even flinch. Steady and fast, she pulled a piece of glass out of the poor animal's paw. She gave it half of her sandwich (then I gave her mine) and off it went to wherever it came from. She's a brave one, this girl. And tall. Not ugly tall like a farm girl, but tall like a Queen or one of those statues you see in museums. With a figure (sorry, Mom, that's for Dad) and knock-out blue eyes. I survived the war and I met someone too. I'm the luckiest guy in the world — I even shouted that up to heaven after I walked her home last night.*

*Ever your loving son, Rory*

*p.s. Her name is Skye. Sky with an E on the end. Skye like the Isle of Skye where she was born.*

# KINCARDINE, 1950

Rory preferred to sit with a bottle of Scotch and listen to "Good Morning Heartache"; she, on the other hand, preferred "Strange Fruit" and a glass of sherry. When Billie Holiday sang the word *drop*, Skye imagined the heat from a southern breeze and although she had never been south, she knew the sweet scent of magnolia intimately. On Saturday mornings they would laze around in their bedclothes and read the newspaper. Then they would put on a record and often, Rory would get in the mood. There was no doubt in Skye's mind that Moira was conceived on the oval carpet in the middle of the front room of the house on Princes Street while Billie sang out...*here is a fruit for the crows to pluck.*

Although Skye knew that she didn't love Rory the way she was supposed to, she enjoyed his long, tight body, his white skin and thick red hair. His leanness was a pleasant shock to her — the soft skin, the flat stomach and the thick, strong, legs. She'd assumed that all men were somewhat like him "down there." Then the Kinsey Report came out and they printed a "reader beware" version of it in the *Toronto Daily Star*.

"Did you know that Alfred Kinsey was a zoologist?" she'd asked him one Sunday morning as he sat reading the Saturday funnies.

"Who's Alfred Kinsey?" he asked. "What's a zool a gist?"

"He did a sex study," she said, tapping her pencil against the newspaper. "There's all kinds of facts here."

"Don't you think it's a little early in the day to be reading smut?"

"Oh my," she blurted out, tapping him on the thigh with the newspaper article about the report. "According to this, I got myself a big one."

Rory's face turned redder than his hair. "Where's our Billie?" he said, slipping out of his pyjamas. "You choose the song."

•

She sighed as she felt her way along the wall of the uterus. The cow moaned but didn't move. Skye hummed, placed her free hand on the exhausted cow's hip. She felt around for the calf's head, then down its spine to the points of its curled up feet.

"A breech birth is no fun for anyone," she told the farmer, who seemed indifferent to her dilemma, preoccupied with sparrows building a nest in the rafters of the barn. Typical of the farmers in the county, he didn't trust that a woman could do the job — especially one from across the ocean.

"Pass me that bale twine," Skye nodded to the floor behind him. "This calf has been dead for a few days."

"I could have gone in there myself," he said, waving his big hands in front of her face. "Except for these; you girls are smaller than men."

"Woman," Skye said. "I haven't been a girl for some time now."

"Woman. Girl. In this country we're not so fussy."

"I'd heard that this country had men in it with manners," she'd said. "Please pass me that string," she asked again. "Or you will have a dead calf *and* a dead cow on your hands."

"Moo," said the farmer. "Moo," he repeated, and dropped the frayed string at her feet before turning to leave the barn.

At first Skye was just happy to be far away from her mother and all the trouble she left behind in Scotland, but eventually she began to miss home, the bulbous rain clouds over the city, the rolling hills and the steep cliff behind the castle, her father's reassuring hand on her shoulder as she studied for her finals.

•

They were both certain it would be a boy, and had given thought to various boys' names — Angus, Carson, Duncan… When the baby turned out to be a girl, they had to rethink their choices — it was Rory who came up with Moira. He'd told her to work past her resentment. "One day your mother will be gone and you'll regret that you've missed your chance."

"I can live with that," Skye said.

"Don't be silly. You sound just like her when you dig your heels in like that."

Skye chuckled at his choice of words, as she was painfully aware that she had been digging her heels into the mattress, probably since the beginning of labour!

"Moira it is, then," Skye sighed, but the instant the words left her mouth, she knew she'd live to regret her decision. "We'll call her Moira," she told him, "but I want a middle name too."

"And what middle name do you have in mind?" he asked, handing back their newborn.

Skye looked down at her daughter, wrapped tightly in the gold silk blanket her mother had sent from Scotland, beautiful with her pink skin and dark eyes. *It's like the one in Dunvegan Castle where you were born*, her mother wrote in the note attached to the blanket. *We can only pray it has the same mystical powers.*

"Her middle name should be Anne. Moira-Anne Rayburn, after my best friend," she said.

•

The day of their wedding in Edinburgh, Anne stood behind Skye doing up her gown.

"You don't love him," she said. "I can tell."

Skye felt herself flush. She faced Anne in her vanity mirror but felt a need to look down and fuss around in her jewellery box.

"Skye," Anne said. "You can call it off, you know."

"How could you suggest such a thing?" Skye said, standing to face her friend.

"Skye, we're best friends, no?"

Skye couldn't talk. She looked at Anne and nodded her head *yes*, and began to cry. Anne held her and she cried until she could finally speak again. "You don't know the half of it," she said, sitting back down in front of the mirror. "I have to get away from Scotland."

"Of course," Anne said, taking her by the shoulders and turning Skye to face her. "I wasn't born yesterday."

Although Anne was only two years older than Skye, she might just as well have been a hundred. Leaving the tenement in East Glasgow where she lived with her mom and her brothers and sisters must have taken courage, but you'd never know it to listen to Anne.

*Never gave it a minute*, she'd said. *Everyone in Scotland knows the Vannan family name.*

"What does it feel like?" Skye asked.

"Skye," Anne asked. "You're a virgin, right?'

Skye looked down for an instant, but then quickly looked back to Anne. "To be really in love?"

Anne placed her hands on Skye's shoulders and looked at her in the vanity mirror.

"You can't stand to be away from him. Not even for a second."

"Oh," Skye said, flattening the front of her gown with her hand. "We'd better not keeping him waiting then."

# KINCARDINE, 1964

The other mothers go to the hairdresser.
*The other mothers go to the hairdresser.*
*The other mothers dress up nice.*
*None of the other mothers smell funny.*

"None of the other mothers *smell funny* …exactly what do you mean by that, Missy?"

"Nothing," Moira said, kicking gravel against the side of the truck.

Skye had stopped on her way from the McCarthy farm to pick Moira up from school. She bit down on her lip, avoided making a comment about the pebbles against her truck.

"Well, none of the other mothers, I'm sure, has spent the last two hours up to her knees in manure trying to steady a colicky horse."

Skye had tried to be gentle. More than anything else in the world, she did not want to become like her mother.

"You are going straight to your room when we get home, young lady," she said, in spite of herself. "And I'll be checking on your homework before you come to the dinner table. Now get in the truck."

"No," Moira said. Just like that.

"Moira," she said, under her breath, aware that the other mothers were listening. "Now," she said, squeezing her daughter's arm, "and no more backtalk."

•

Skye had tried to stop being resentful of her parents — they never came to Canada to see her. From time to time she would receive a wire with money, but only with the briefest note from her mother with instructions for how it should be spent.

*For Moira's winter coat and boats.*
*For Moira's tutor, and tuition for a proper teacher.*
*Fare to send my namesake HOME to meet her grandparents.*

Skye sent the money back with a note: *We're doing perfectly well with finances, Mother...besides, it's too far a journey for a young girl to make on her own.*

No one needed to make that horrific journey across the ocean; Skye felt nauseated at the mere thought of a boat.

# KINCARDINE, 1965

"It's my job, Moira," Skye told her. "It's my job to get messy and yes, sometimes by the end of the day, I look and smell like a sickly cow or horse."

It was Sunday afternoon and they had stopped at the Farmers' Market. Skye had been called to look in on a colicky thoroughbred and she'd picked up Moira at the beach before stopping at the market. Several of the mothers were there, a group of them on their way back from church.

"Well you could have at least changed your top," Moira whispered, pointing to a manure stain on her shirt.

"And you should watch how you talk to me," Skye said. "I am your mother after all. I've been spinning like a fly with one wing since the crack of dawn today."

"See what I mean?" said Moira, looking over at the other mothers and raising her voice. "Everything is about animals. What is *spinning like a fly with one wing* supposed to mean?"

"I'm busy, Moira. That's what that expression means," Skye said, looking over at the other mothers, and raising her voice as well. "I don't have time to sit in a beauty parlour and gossip all day."

Skye knew that she had crossed a line and regretted it immediately. But it was too late to retract what she said; Moira had already thrown her swimming towel on the ground and stomped away. Fifteen is a rough time for girls — Skye knew this only too well. She'd hated fifteen and sixteen and seventeen. She hurried to catch up to her daughter at the truck.

"I'm sorry," she said. "I shouldn't have yelled. And, yes, I could have made myself up a little — I'll try harder to make you proud of me."

"I *am* proud of you, Mother," Moira said. "Bet you can't say the same about me."

Skye didn't know what to say, so she remained silent. She stared at her daughter, who looked as though she would burst into tears. She knew she should hug her and tell her that she loved her and that, of course, she was very proud of her, but she didn't.

"Let's get over to the strawberries before they're all gone," she said. "They say it's the best year yet for sweet and plump."

# KINCARDINE, 1966

When Moira met Magnus, Skye found it impossible to hide her disappointment. Moira brought him by the house after school one September afternoon. He was on the soccer team.

"He's somewhat short," Skye told Moira after he'd gone.

"Height isn't everything," Rory said, standing to leave the kitchen where the four of them had been eating cupcakes. "I think this is a mother-to-daughter discussion."

"Short is good for soccer," Moira said. "They have a good centre of gravity, right, Dad?"

"I'm staying out of this one," Rory said, putting his hand over his mouth as he walked away.

"What does his father do for a living?" Skye asked.

"How should I know? I didn't ask."

"Well, have you been to their house?"

"Yes, I have been to their house, Mother, and it's a dump — is that what you want to hear? They're poor. They're from the rotten side of Barrie. Poverty is in his blood."

"Poverty isn't genetic," Skye told her. "Expectations of those with less is, however, passed down through the generations."

"What about rich people?" Moira asked. "Is snobbery *passed down* too, Mother?"

Skye hit the roof. Before grounding Moira, she yelled loud enough to bring Rory back into the kitchen.

"I've fought snobbery," she said. "I've resisted elitist attitudes my entire life. Don't pull the snobbery line on me, Missy. You're grounded for two weeks!"

"That punishment is a little severe," Rory said, that night as they lay side-by-side in bed. "And did you hear what you called her?"

Skye was facing the wall, still fuming, and he was doing his best to calm her down, but not successfully.

"I called her by her name and you were no help, Rory Rayburn. The things that come out of that girl's mouth are completely disrespectful of me, and you don't step in to help."

"She's not that bad, Skye. She's a normal teenage girl, from what I can see of other girls her age in this community. You called her *Missy*."

"That's the problem," said Skye, ignoring the *Missy* part of Rory's statement. "She's running around with the riffraff instead of focussing on her studies. She'll never get accepted to university at the rate she's going. And god only knows what she's up to with that boy."

"Somewhat of a rebel, isn't she?" Rory said, gently tickling her in the ribs. "Remind you of anyone we know?"

"Not me," Skye snapped, pushing his hand away. "Had I talked to my mother the way Moira talks to me, I would have been disinherited and thrown into the street."

"That's an exaggeration," Rory said. "Your mother was strict, but she loved you. And Moira, well she has a spirit, but she just wants you to like her — maybe you could try a little."

"*Like her?* She's my daughter. It's natural, I don't have to try to *like her*," Skye said, sitting up and turning on the bedside light, knocking her miniature Ganesha to the floor. She looked down at the statue — the elephant with hands for feet and many arms, dancing on its lotus flower base.

Ganesha had become a symbol of hope to her, a reminder of her father's gentle nature, but more importantly a symbol of possibility and new beginnings. Her father gave it to her the morning she boarded the ship from Scotland. *It's a new day*, he told her, handing her the small brass statue. *I bought it in Calcutta and it has brought me luck all these years. You're off now to create a legacy of your own. And I know you will*," he said, kissing her cheek. *You are a force of nature, Skye, and you come by your disposition naturally*, nodding in the direction of her mother, who was sobbing in the back seat of the car. Skye knew so little about her parents. At first she was glad that her mother had stayed in the car, but as her father walked away, Skye would have given anything for a word of encouragement from her.

*Walk like a lady. You're gangly as a giraffe.*

Skye stood tall and walked toward the ship where Rory was waiting.

She got out of bed and picked the statue off the bedroom floor and held it in the palm of her hand.

"What are you thinking?" Rory asked her, rubbing her back.

"I'm thinking about Anne, all those years working for Mother and Dad. She'd moved to Edinburgh to have a better life — all those years washing the floors and scrubbing soup pots and toilets. I'm thinking you might just be right."

"About your parents?"

"About Moira."

"Turn out the light and come back to bed," Rory said.

"In a minute," she said, placing the dancing Ganesha back on the night table. "I need to spend a few minutes with my daughter."

•

Skye had every intention of apologizing. She would speak to Moira in a calm voice, and she would take away her punishment. She tiptoed down the hallway to her daughter's room and looked for light coming from under the door, but there was none. She debated whether or not to disturb her, but decided, in the end, that it would be worth waking Moira because she would be so pleased to learn that she was no longer grounded. She tapped on the door lightly at first, but when there was no answer, she knocked a little louder. When there still was no answer, Skye cracked open the door and looked into the room. "Moira," she whispered. "Are you asleep?"

## SQUIRREL

| Species | Sciurus carolinensis |
|---|---|
| Phylum | Chordata |
| Order | Rodentia |
| Family | Sciuridae |
| Description | Pointed face, dark eyes and whiskers; claws on their feet and tufts of hair on their small ears. On average, they are 60–70 centimetres long, not counting the bushy tail. |
| Attributes | None — they are persistent and bothersome rodents. |

Life Lesson for Duncan

Don't take prisoners.

# KINCARDINE, 1981

Rory made friends in town, she didn't. It wasn't that a few people didn't welcome her, invite her to tea or for a meal, she was just never very good at small talk. He, on the other hand, loved chatting with people and wanted to know more about all aspects of their lives. He was particularly interested in a person who had an accent. *Where are you from?* Rory would ask. *Oh? And what part of Germany* (or France, or India, or …) *is that?* He would find out what foods they liked and what schools they'd attended. He would remember the names of their children, their ages, and what they were interested in becoming when they grew up. She, on the other hand, would remember the name of their pet.

Of all the symptoms of Rory's cancer, it was the depression that Skye couldn't make sense of. He used to be so outgoing and happy.

*You go*, he'd say, if she suggested a walk on the beach. *Not tonight*, he'd tell her, if she suggested driving into town for an ice cream.

The weight loss came on suddenly and it soon became undeniable that something serious was going on.

"It's not like you've decreased your food intake or become more physically active," she'd said. "As a matter of fact, you've become utterly and completely lethargic. Please help me plug up that hole in the attic where the squirrel gets in," she'd asked. "Do you think there's some way we can cut down the tree that's leaning against the house?"

Of course Rory would never have anything to do with cutting down a tree, even if he'd had the strength to swing an axe. Keeping a squirrel out of the attic, on the other hand, would have been a pleasurable challenge for him.

"I'll plug up the hole later," he said. "I'm sure I can reach it from our bedroom window."

The morning Rory passed away, Skye stayed in bed. She held his hand and touched his face. The physical signs of death were explicit and cruel. So insistent was the pale blue complexion. So telling was the cold skin of his once strong hands. She moved closer to her husband. The silence comforted her. No cars rolling up Princes Street. No birds in the tree near the house. No squirrel noises in the attic above her head; no scratching then scampering across the floor. She thought back to Edinburgh. How she met Rory in the rain — their first date at Arthur's Seat; the stray dog with a thorn in its paw; the flock of cormorants that flew overhead when they kissed the very first time. He adored and trusted her, never seemed worried that she would go with another man and she never worried that his eye would roam to someone younger or content to be sitting at home with knitting needles instead of traipsing across Bruce County to birth a cow in the middle of the night.

There were too many wives in the area who had no place to turn with their worries. They didn't trust each other, and they didn't want Skye too close to their husbands.

"He hasn't touched me for two months," one wife said, glaring at her and wiping flour onto her apron.

"You can take your hands off your hips," Skye said, noticing the diamond on the woman's blistered hands covered with pastry and flour. "I'm not interested in your husband."

"Three hours to birth a cow? I'm not stupid," the woman said.

Skye tried not to make a joke that might parallel the cow and the ample woman, standing in front of her, red-faced and near tears.

"A caesarian and twins is no two-minute job," she said.

"In the far barn?"

"I don't choose the barn. I go where I'm told."

"Get out then," she said pointing to the door. The woman's anger was frightening and forceful — her shaking fist, squinting red face, stomping feet and fierce words. "I'll tell you where to go. Get out!"

"Interesting tactic," Skye said, staying calm, holding her hand out. "I need to be paid for my work."

"Go get it from him!" the woman said, nodding in the direction of the barn. Lowering her voice, sounding somewhat defeated, she added a halfhearted: "I'm sure you gave him what he wanted."

Skye was well aware of the impact she had on some people. She was tall and slim and had been told on more than one occasion that with her bone structure and *those eyes* she could easily be a big city model. She was aware that she commanded a certain authority in town and some people resented that. This crossed the line though. The implication that she was a prostitute was too much.

"You get out there and stand in blood and urine and pull out a near dead calf. You get out to the barn and deal with your husband's foul mouth and bad breath and standing too close no matter how many times you ask him to stand back. And you better think long and hard the next time your bull scours or your dumb cow has swallowed something off the barn floor and you need my help to get it out."

The wife's face softened and she turned her back on Skye. She pulled a sewing tin down from a shelf above the stove. Skye could see a few bills under pieces of cloth and clumps of thread with pins and needles stuck in them. People's happiness depended on lots of things — family, home…but mostly, it depended on their ability to stand up for themselves. There were too many people on this earth who just couldn't muster the strength to stand when they were being pushed down.

"I believe you," she said, handing Skye a handful of bills. "Sorry."

Skye set the money down on the kitchen table and faced the woman.

"The twins are underweight," she said. "Keep your eye on them for a day or two."

"Doctor Rayburn?" the woman said.

"Yes?"

"Oh, never mind," she said. "I'll figure it out."

"Does your husband know about that tin?" Skye asked from the doorway.

The woman untied her apron and dropped it on a chair. She took the money off the table and put it back into the tin. "I don't think so," she said.

"I'd keep it that way," said Skye.

It wasn't her style to come right out and give advice, but she always found a way of planting a seed. The wife's intuition about the husband and prostitutes was dead on. Everyone in town knew it. Everyone knew that the marriage was no good. Everyone knew that the husband didn't need to drive into Toronto to buy new boots or a power saw every Sunday after church.

The next time Skye saw the wife she was working at the Canadian Tire off Highway 21. She pretended not to know her at first, but eventually the woman came over.

"Can I help you find something?" she asked.

"I need some thick, firm wire …" Skye said, "…for a breech calf near Purple Grove."

As she handed her a spool of thick electrical wire, Skye noticed that the woman's hands were still red, but there was no ring. No diamond crusted with lard and flour. No rage in the woman's face.

"Sometimes the dead calf's parts get stuck inside," Skye told her.

"Yuck," the woman said.

"Yes," said Skye. "That's a good word for it."

She took a solemn oath. Made a promise to watch over animals and relieve their suffering. *How could you?* Skye asked herself, looking up through the mesh into the dark.

# KINCARDINE, 1982

The day Duncan was born, Magnus got drunk. Skye knocked on the door where he and Moira lived at the Royal Apartments and when no one answered, she walked right in. Not only was the door unlocked, it had been left slightly open. Skye knelt beside Magnus, who was passed out on the floor, to hear his breathing and to feel his pulse. She could smell his gin-soaked breath. He was clammy, but his heartbeat was steady. Short and wiry, strong as a horse, he'd be all right. She dropped his wrist and tried to coax him to consciousness with strong words and a glass of cold water. Then she squatted next to him. She slid one arm under his legs, and the other behind his back and lifted him off the kitchen floor. Skye carried him, inch by inch, down the hallway. She didn't want Moira to see him like this. She lowered him onto the living room sofa, brushed her hands and puffed up her chest: *not so bad for an old girl,* she was thinking when Moira walked into the room with her blue blanket bundle in her arms. Magnus knew they'd be home from the hospital by two o'clock. He was supposed to make up the baby's bed with fresh sheets and drape the crib with the gold blanket — the same silk cover that her mother had sent Moira from Scotland, the one with mystical powers like the Fairy Flag she was born beside at Dunvegan castle. Instead, he drank. *The boys just kept the cigars and shots coming,* he told them when he woke up late that evening. *Cut me some slack, Moira,* he pleaded. *It's just what proud fathers do.* He'd turned his back to Skye, but she could see them kiss in the mirror above the sofa and knew that she should leave the lovebirds to make up — there'd be another fight soon enough. Skye didn't understand the attraction; Moira had all kinds of decent boys tripping over her when she was a young girl. She and Magnus had been together for sixteen years, Skye couldn't believe they'd just had their first child.

"Let's take a picture," Skye said, raising her Polaroid camera. Moira held Duncan close to her breast. Magnus leaned into his wife and son, struggling, it seemed to keep his eyes open.

•

Skye felt as though a missing piece had flown back to her. Duncan was a handsome child who didn't fuss the way Moira did when she was a baby.

"He's perfect," she told Moira. "And," nodding at Magnus, who was sipping coffee in a chair pushed back from the bed, "handsome like his father."

They wanted a home birth, but there were complications. *Irregular heartbeat and very, very small,* said Doctor Roth at Moira's seven-month examination.

"I'll take a sip of that," said Moira, nodding at her husband's coffee, trying to regain her strength after a rough delivery two days earlier.

Magnus hesitated, but held out the cup to her.

"It has a drop of brandy in it," he said.

"You're kidding?" Moira said, more sad than angry. "It's eight o'clock in the morning."

"Hair of the dog that bit ya," said Magnus, setting the cup on the night table and taking the baby from her.

"I'm walking down to the store," Skye said. "Would either of you like something from the store?"

"That's a little far from here, Mother," Moira said, sipping the brandied coffee.

"Not really," said Skye. "The walk will do me good."

# PART II

# KINCARDINE, 1984

If she told him once, she'd told him a thousand times: "Magnus Johnson, what's done is done and I'm not the one to judge you. The boy needs a father," she'd said.

"I know, Skye," Magnus said, nodding his head up and down.

It was a few months after Moira had died and they were standing on the sidewalk in front of the Princes Street house. Magnus was late to pick up Duncan and Skye had to get to work, it was spring and there seemed to be an unusual number of complicated births among the livestock. Duncan was waiting on the steps of the house. She attempted to keep her voice down, but her anger had control of the better part of her logic.

"Kids need guidance. None of them are born naturally good," she whispered, surprised by her choice of words — actually, her mother's words. "It's thankless work, the job of raising children; you need to be steady and calm," Skye told Magnus.

"The way you were with Moira?"

After the car accident Skye would take Duncan for a day or two at a time. She said it was so Magnus could have a little time to himself, but she knew better, the writing was on the wall — her son-in-law had survived the crash, but the guilt was eating him alive.

"Sorry," he said.

Magnus had promised to be a proper dad — stop drinking, start looking for work. And he'd meant it every time. He'd stay sober for a day or two. Sometimes he'd make it to the shower to get cleaned up and head out the door for an interview. His dark hair slicked back and wearing a clean white shirt, he looked like a boy being sent off for school. But he'd never make it to the interview. He walked with dignity down Princes to Queen Street where he'd stop for a beer at the Bruce Inn. One pint to cut the nerves, another pint to block out the image of Moira, dead in the car, that kept popping up in his head; a third because he saw Squirrely Shirley on the other side of the bar in a short skirt and tube top that only went partway over her boobs.

Skye figured that her son-in-law was no different than the unemployed men of her youth in Scotland. Same trouble. Different continent. Sometimes they grew out of their grief or recklessness and sometimes they didn't. Rory hadn't lived long enough to see his first grandson, but he would have known what to say. Man-to-man, he might have helped Magnus shake off the guilt. Man-to-man, there may have been some hope.

"What's done is done," she repeated. "If ever your son needs a proper father, it's now."

•

"Walls don't exist for children like Duncan," Skye told him.

It was a few weeks after Magnus had returned, and two days before he'd leave Kincardine again for good. They were putting Duncan to bed.

"That was dumb of me to leave," he whispered to Skye. "I promise to work at being a good dad. I just feel crappy about the drinking in the car and stuff."

Skye didn't want to hear it again. Magnus would have to learn to live with himself, a new life was taking shape, Duncan was walking now and learning to articulate his words. *Bir bir.*

"They walk through brick and float through windows with their imaginations," said Skye.

"But there's nothing there," said Magnus, pointing to the ceiling above Duncan's bed, "and he keeps pointing up there."

*Bir bir. Bir bir.*

•

*Bird* was the first word he learned. Duncan and Skye were sitting in the uncut grass behind the Princes Street house. *Bir Bir*, he said, pointing to a pair of blue jays fighting with a crow who had invaded the apple tree.

"Yes, Duncan," she'd said. "Those are birds."

She could sit with him for hours like this. Him crawling around her, trying to stand, falling back into the grass and crying until she'd pick him up.

*Bir bir*, he said again. Then he said something that sent shivers up and down her spine. *Ma ma*, he said. *Ma ma*, he repeated, pointing to the upstairs window of the house.

"Oh sweet boy," she said, hugging him tightly. "Ma ma is not there."

But he wouldn't stop. He kept repeating the words and pointing. *Ma ma ma ma ma ma*. And after a while, she picked him up and carried him into the house.

She set him on the kitchen floor and started to prepare lunch, but he'd continued to cry: *Ma ma ma ma*, he said, pointing to the stairs. Skye lifted him up and he stopped crying. She carried him up the stairs trying to calm him down. "Maybe you've had too much sun, sweet boy," she said. "Time for your nap."

When she placed him on the bed, he continued to cry. *Ma ma*, he said, looking at the chair next to the bed. *Ma ma*, he repeated.

When Moira was born, Skye's mother told her not to pick her up once she'd been put down to sleep.

*What if she needs to feed?* she had asked her mother.

*All they want is attention when they cry like that. I never picked you up once when you cried at night*, her mother said, proudly.

The window was open and there was a warm, fragrant breeze. Skye thought about the pink and white roses that grew wild along the beach. She walked over to the bed and picked Duncan up as well as the gold blanket he refused to let go of. She sat in the chair that he'd been pointing to and hummed Hey Diddle Diddle, Moira's favourite nursery rhyme, while he fell asleep, staring at something she couldn't see.

## HORSE

| | |
|---|---|
| Species | Equus ferus caballus |
| Phylum | Chordata |
| Order | Perissodactyla |
| Family | Equidae |
| Description | Long neck with a mane and strong, slender legs; a single toe on each foot. |
| Attributes | Excellent sight and hearing, they can run at high speeds. |

*Life Lesson for Duncan*
*Gallop is better than canter. Fight is better than flight.*

# KINCARDINE, 1989

For his seventh birthday, Skye brought home a puppy for Duncan. "It's a Scottish terrier," she said, handing him the growling pup. "Someone was selling the litter from a box in the parking lot behind the Sunrise Grill."

The Sunset Grill was on one side of the street and the Sunrise Grill on the other; Duncan got confused about which was which. He took the puppy from Skye; its fur was white and prickly.

"It's a boy," said Skye. "What would you like to call him?"

"But we already have a dog," Duncan said.

"Well," said Skye. "Rocky will have a little friend now."

Duncan blurted out: "Thistle. Let's call him Thistle. Like the weed you told me about from back *hoome*," he says, trying to imitate her Scottish accent.

"Aye," Skye said. "That's very clever. Thistle it is then."

That night as the pup slept in a wicker basket by his bed, Duncan took out his notebook and a piece of grey charcoal. He drew the prickly fur and the pointed ears. He drew the pink tongue hanging out of its mouth. When Skye crept into his room early the next morning to take the puppy out for his morning walk, she saw the drawing on the floor by the bed.

As they sat at the breakfast table, she studied the perfectly rendered drawing. "How is this possible?" she asked her grandson. "You're but seven years old."

"I don't know," Duncan said.

"But it's far too advanced for your age."

"I just did it like I saw."

"Show me then," Skye insisted. "Draw a picture of Rocky."

And he did. Duncan drew Rocky and Thistle. He drew the squirrel climbing a tree and the feral cat under the back porch. Where did this come from? Skye asked herself. That child's talent with animals is uncanny.

"What's drunk, Grandma Skye?" he asked, looking down at his feet dangling over the wooden chair.

"Drunk?" Skye pulled her chair close to her grandson's, hardly able to breathe. "Why do you ask?"

Duncan dropped the charcoal and pointed to the front door. His face turned red and Skye could see that he was about to cry. "They said at Fincher's my dad's a drunk and he killed my mom."

●

"Canter," said Skye. "Canter, not gallop."

"What's the difference?" Duncan asked.

"A canter is refined," she said. "A gallop is erratic and out of control."

"I'm tired," Duncan said. "I don't want to play anymore."

"Finally," said Skye. "Let's get you to bed then."

From the minute he could walk, Duncan was what Skye called *high spirited*. Although he was shy and introverted, he never sat still long enough to eat a proper meal. He never slept through the night and often woke with nightmares. So every evening, Skye did her best to tire him out.

In the bedroom, Duncan slowly undressed. He waited until she turned her back before slipping off his swimsuit and putting on his pyjamas.

When Skye turned back around, Duncan was in bed, staring up at the ceiling.

"There's something living in the roof," he said, matter-of-factly.

"There's a squirrel up there," Skye said.

"But it's not the squirrel. I saw it once."

"You saw what?" Skye asked, pulling the blankets up around his neck.

Duncan hesitated, his brown eyes tearing. "It had pointed teeth like a shark and eyes like an eagle."

"And you have a big imagination!" she said.

"It was for real, Grandma Skye," he said, frowning.

"Sharks need water," she said. "Or else they die. You know that."

"It had teeth like a shark but it was a horse."

Skye had had enough of horses for one day. She'd spent several hours at one barn floating the teeth of four horses. Horses' teeth grow constantly and the lower jaw is narrower than the upper, so out she went to Walkerton with her eighteen-inch bar with a rasp on the end. The first three horses weren't difficult, but the fourth reared up and lunged, coming down hard on her left shoulder. *Sedation time*, she'd told the owner. And after a few minutes the horse settled down enough for her to reach in and grab its tongue, pull it to one side, and rasp the teeth even.

"Maybe you can draw a picture of it sometime, sweet boy?" she said. "But right now, you need to go to sleep."

"I drew one already," he said, kicking back the bed cover.

"Well, that's good then," she said, pulling the gold blanket up over his chest again. "That's a good use of your imagination."

Duncan kicked the cover off. "It's not my imagination," he said. "I saw it."

"No, you don't," she said, pulling the cover back up. Then she remembered a similar battle when Moira was a child. The battle at bedtime was endless with her. *You're not going to win this one, Missy,* she'd tell Moira. *Push back these blankets one more time and you can go stand in the corner with no blanket at all and see what that's like. This blanket is magic...sent all the way from Scotland.*

"Have your way then, child," she said. "But if you get cold in the night, bundle up."

Duncan looked over to his grandmother as she stood by his bedroom door.

"Do dogs go to heaven?" he'd asked, looking over at Thistle, asleep in his basket at the foot of the bed. "Even bad dogs?"

"I don't see why not," Skye answered, lowering her voice to a whisper. "Thistle is sleeping like a good little dog."

"Grandma Skye," he said in a quiet voice. "Do you think you might die someday like my mom?"

"Oh, dear God," she said, almost falling over. "I assume so, sweet boy, but I hope not for a very, very long time."

"Do you think it would be okay to keep on the light just for tonight?"

Skye felt her way back through the dark and sat on the edge of his bed.

"You have Thistle," she said, but could tell he wasn't comforted by her suggestion that the sleeping pup could somehow be a guard dog.

"What if your horse were a friendly horse? A mighty horse with kind, dark eyes. Would you still be afraid of the dark?"

"Maybe," he said.

"And that horse could take you any place you liked — a place with light, even in the night. An imaginary island surrounded by blue water and toothless sharks."

Duncan laughed. "Toothless sharks. How could they eat?"

"They're imaginary, they don't need to eat," she said, walking back to the door.

"Anywhere? The horse can fly anywhere?"

"It's your magic horse," Skye whispered, flicking on the light. "As a matter of fact," she added, "it could be like the creature from Loch Ness — a sea horse that can dive deep into the water."

"What's a loch, Grandma?" he asked.

"A lake, dear boy. Loch means the same as lake."

"So that's Loch Huron," said Duncan, pointing out the window.

"Loch Huron, indeed," Skye said.

The squirrel scampered along thin branches. It climbed over sheds and up stucco walls. It ate the food it found in trash cans or fallen fruit from the apple tree. Occasionally there was no food to be found.

*Come here, little squirrel,* Duncan said. *Don't be afraid.*

He pulled a chair across the floor and used it to prop the screen door open. He stood where it could see him, a cracker with peanut butter in his hand. The squirrel inched closer; the smell of peanuts drew it in. It looked all around the room, then scampered a few inches forward.

*Come here, Brownie,* Duncan said. *It's peanut butter.*

He sat on the kitchen floor with the peanut butter cracker in his held-out hand. He told the squirrel everything. He talked about how he too could climb and fly. He told the squirrel that he would like to live with it and jump from branch to branch through the sky: *if that's all right?* He talked about his dead mother and how he hated cars. He said his father was missing, lost in the city. And sometimes he talked to the squirrel about Skye. *She's a doctor,* he told her. *My grandma acts silly like a kid and fixes sick animals.*

The squirrel seemed to be listening for noises coming from the street or for the sound of feet on the porch. It ate until the door slammed closed. It jumped to the counter, then to the curtain above the sink. Duncan said *it's just wind. It's okay, Brownie,* he said, *don't be scared.* But there was a shadow in the doorway and a broom thrashing about the room as the squirrel flew out the door. *They're full of fleas and disease,* Skye yelled at Duncan. *They're not meant to be inside a house.*

●

"Beavers are stupid," Duncan said. "Why can't we have something neat like an eagle?"

"Because the Americans have the eagle," Skye answered, feeling more and more exasperated. "Now, enough questions for one day."

Duncan held the nickel to her face. She was on the sofa trying to nap, but it was raining and he was bored.

"It's ugly," he said, imitating beaver teeth by sticking two fingers in the front of his mouth.

Skye tried not to laugh, but he saw her. He took a magazine from the coffee table and held it on his bottom, flapped it like a stiff tail.

"And his stupid tail is even uglier than its face," he said.

"Beavers were important to the economic development of Canada," she said, rolling onto her side and pulling the pillow over her head. "Now let me sleep for a few minutes. Please."

"How?" he asked.

"Duncan," Skye said, raising her voice slightly. "I will tell you this one thing and then I need to rest."

"Well?" he said, flopping down on the sofa by her feet.

"Well," she said, sitting up. "Canada's cod and her forests were important, but the fur traders were responding to a fashion — beaver hats were very big for women and men."

"Gross," he said. "A beaver on your head."

"Yes," Skye said. "*Gross*, but in demand. There used to be millions of beavers here, but one hundred thousand pelts were shipped to Europe each year."

"But you said they're rodents. Like rats and squirrels."

"They are, Duncan," she said. "But just because an animal is a rodent doesn't mean that its fur isn't desirable. I had one of those hats once."

"Yuck," he said. "Why do we have zoos?" he asked, standing in front of her.

"Duncan?" she said. "The deal was I would answer one question and then you would let me nap. I have to go back to work soon."

"Okay," he said, looking down at his feet. "Go to sleep, Grandma Skye."

But Skye was wide awake and his question was one she had grappled with. Zoos had never been her favourite places and Duncan had been pleading with her for several months to take him to the Toronto zoo.

"They are sort of like museums," she said, "usually for city people."

"Boring."

"A place where animals can be observed."

"Like in the wild?" he'd asked, becoming more excited.

Duncan had told her on several occasions that he wanted to see the lions and monkeys. He also wanted to see bats and snakes.

"Somewhat," she said. "But animals change in captivity."

"How?"

"They just do," she said.

The day they went to the zoo, Duncan gathered up his sketchbook and the allowance he'd saved to buy the animals treats. They took the bus from Kincardine to Toronto, and then the subway across the city. Then they took another bus and waited in line to get in. Duncan had been awake most of the night; Skye could hear him pacing, saw the light go on and off from under his door. He was too excited to eat breakfast; she could hardly get him to wash his face and comb his hair.

"Boring," he said, looking at the lions in the cage. "Where is he?" he said about the baboon. "Is it dead?" he asked about the snake curled up in the corner of an overly-lit aquarium.

The orang-utan house was much more interesting to Duncan. A female made a bed out of straw. Using her arms like legs, she moved gracefully across the cage.

"She's just like a real person," he said, pointing. "Look, she's walking sideways."

As if on cue, the orang-utan looked at the two of them — Duncan, who was still pointing, and Skye, who was in tears.

"What's wrong, Grandma Skye?" he'd asked.

The orang-utan sat against the glass of the cage. She had her baby under one arm. She was gentle with him; tender and loving in the way she held him.

"The baby is like an ugly little kid," Duncan said. "Will it survive?"

"Why do you ask that?" Skye said.

"Because it's in a cage."

"She'll probably survive."

"It's a boy," said Duncan, blushing. "I saw."

"I'm talking about the mother," said Skye. "Sometimes the mother dies in captivity."

The mother orang-utan pressed the baby's head against her breast. The baby wiggled out of her arms and sauntered over to them. Duncan kept his face pressed against the glass. Skye stepped back. The mother advanced, nonchalantly, and picked up her young.

"Let's go," Skye said.

She took Duncan by hand and led him away. Her eyes. The orang-utan had closed her eyes, and the lids were transparent as porcelain. When she opened those watery, brown eyes again, Skye recognized an expression in them — not fear or desperation; rather a look of resignation that Skye could hardly bear to look at.

Skye explained the art of baking crow's feet pie. Moira was never interested in being domestic, but to Skye's delight, unlike his mother, Duncan always wanted to be in the kitchen with her while she baked.

"You prepare the wet ingredients first," she said. "Blueberries, ripe as you can get 'em, blue-black off the branch so they're practically still growing."

It was a rainy Sunday morning; they sat at the kitchen table. With flour on his shirt and blueberries on his hands and cheeks, Duncan looked up at her with bewildered eyes.

"Add raspberries, juicy and bright, plump with rain. No cornstarch. No sugar, nothing but the natural juices and a squeeze of lemon. Any good pie needs a little tart," she said, squeezing his cheek. "That's the crow in crow's feet pie."

"That's it?" Duncan asked. "No real feet?"

"The crow's feet are these little lines under your grandmother's eyes," she said, pointing to her wrinkles; then she bent over to untie his running shoe, "when she takes a big mouthful of the pie and her whole mouth lifts up and she's halfway to heaven with a bit of the sun and earth inside."

"That's it?" he'd asked again. "No real crow's feet. Or at least some worms or toes or something."

"Well," Skye said, looking down at her rough old hands, rubbing them together. "There is a story, but let me tell you how to make the pastry first."

"Sure," he said.

"The trick of making pastry, sweet boy," she said, "is to not push and pound it too much. Mix your flour, lard and water, then add a pinch of salt and a sprinkle of vinegar, just knead it two or three times and set it aside. Flour your pie plate and press down with your big finger, the thumb's print is important," she said, pressing her thumb into his forehead to make her point.

"Fold in the innards, the colour of a pinched-arm bruise, then roll out your top. Flatten it thin. Then flatten it again. Use your fork to make ridges like crow's claw marks all along the ridges. Carve out your bird freehand, from memory of the last crow you saw, and then make slits in the crust to let the blueberry juices boil out; the sugar from the berries will brown the crust."

"*Now* can I get the real story?" he asked, kicking the underside of the table with his one shoe. "The one with crow's feet, not stupid blueberries."

"Crow's feet are a delicacy," she said. And leaning across the table, added: "Crows are a sacred mix of love and wisdom, with a dash of worry and a sprinkle of battle thrown in. The wrong pie to the wrong boy can cause madness, even death — like giving the MacDonalds a pie baked by the MacLeods. Now give me that other shoe," she said. "Time to get you into the bathtub. Time to tickle those toes and scrub these dirty little knees."

CROW

| Species | Corvus brachyrhynchos |
| --- | --- |
| Phylum | Chordata |
| Order | Passeriformes |
| Family | Corvidae |
| Description | Black legs, feet and talons; black bill; black eyes; blue-black feathers. |
| Attributes | Smart. Really, really smart and wicked. Crows are highly intelligent, masterful hunters. Tricksters and subjects of myth, crows are reputed to have perfect vision. |

Life Lesson for Duncan

Be careful what you ask for: you might get it.

# KINCARDINE, 1990

Thistle used to play as Rocky tried to sleep. He'd bite at Rocky's ears and bark in his face. Rocky would groan and stretch and try to ignore the smaller dog. Rocky'd had a good run on the beach and added his scent to every other trash bag on Princes Street. He growled and stretched his long, black legs; Skye felt the weight of his lovely head on her feet. She'd hoped that Duncan would take an interest in taking care of Thistle, but he didn't. Maybe, just maybe he would be interested in going to Cornell one day, follow in her footsteps? But Duncan's interest in animals seemed deeper than medicine.

"He's your pet, Duncan," she said. "You need to take care of him."

"But how can he be mine? You can't own an animal."

Skye thought about what he said.

"You're Thistle's guardian," she said. "It's a responsibility."

"But you can't own a living thing," Duncan insisted.

Skye was shocked by his insistence. There wasn't much else to say, so she sat and watched him sketch Thistle. His drawings were detailed and accurate, more like photographs than a young child's art. And as she thought about them, she realized that the drawings were like the illustrations that she once did as a veterinarian student — there was energy around the animal, and movement. *Focus on your studies*, her mother threatened. *Enough doodling and daydreaming. Remember, you have one year to prove yourself.*

"You're right, darling boy," she conceded. And out of the ether, an image of Magnus crowded her thoughts. "You can't own a living thing."

Duncan knew from the time he was little that there was magic in everything; the grass, trees, stars and wind contained secrets. Nature was alive in ways that grownups didn't notice — everything had a colour around it — green, gold or blue around people, pink or red around plants and animals. He stopped telling his teacher about what he could see when she'd send him home with a note. Skye asked him what he'd said to alarm his teacher, but she didn't wait for his answer. She took his face in her hands and looked in his eyes: *We all have secrets, there are certain things that we keep to ourselves.*

Everything was ecstatic and leaping — toads and rabbits, birds and butterflies moved to beams of sunlight. Duncan would sit in the backyard garden on Princes Street for hours. It was easy for him to hide in the uncut grass and flowers. He was eight years old and Skye had gone to the store for milk. *Five minutes,* she'd told him, kissing the top of his head. She brought him a pad of paper and his crayons and instructed him to draw the pretty black birds. *Don't you dare step a foot outside this yard.* The wind, blowing in trees, sounded the same as the waves on the lake when he closed his eyes. He liked the way the flowers smelled and he was glad that he wasn't afraid of bees the way some of the kids at school were. Skye told him that the orange butterflies were called monarchs and that they travel far — all the way to Mexico. He shook a crayon from the box and slowly drew a large purple wing. He drew the other wing, trying to make it the same size, then he added a small pink body in the middle. He wondered what it would be like to be so little and still be able to fly so far. In his mind, he rode through the air. He closed his eyes and floated up through the trees with white blossoms, above the yard with all the grass and flowers and over the street lined with houses. He could see the whole town and the giant lake that looked green instead of blue the way he was told water is supposed to be. He hovered above the shore at the edge of the town where there were boulders in the water and fallen trees. Once he reached the nuclear plant he flew back over his school and the church. He saw Skye going into Fincher's and then to Macs; she was wearing her red top and shorts. Her arms were long and strong like some of the fathers', and her legs were tall like a giraffe's. He waited until she got back into the car, then he flew back over the houses on their street. Then, hidden by the flowers and the tall grass, he slept and dreamt of elephants. When he opened his eyes the trees were swaying like clouds and Skye was kneeling beside him with an ice cream cone in her hand.

# KINCARDINE, 1991

**D**uncan loved anything with wings. He made his toy truck fly as if it were an airplane. He flew his tin soldier like a sparrow, up and down through the imaginary clouds of his bedroom.

"It seems that everything in this room gets to fly except your airplanes," Skye said, standing behind him. Duncan dropped the soldier on the floor and swivelled on his knees to face her.

"Oh," he said, as he pushed his tin soldier back and forth, making car engine noises.

"I think you're confused, dear boy," she said. "Trucks move across the ground, soldiers walk and airplanes fly."

Duncan didn't speak. He continued to pretend that the soldier was a truck. Skye sat on the floor beside him.

"Ouff," she said. "It's getting hard for your old gran to get up and down."

Duncan handed her the pillow from under his knees without looking up from his tin man truck.

"Thank you," she said. "Did I ever tell you about the owl your granddad and I saw in Scotland?"

Duncan shook his head no.

"Well," she said. "It was something else. We were at Arthur's Seat, waaaayy up at the top ..."

"What's Arthur's Seat?" he asked.

"It's in Edinburgh," she said. "It's a famous hill where you can see all over the city in one direction and out across the country in the other."

"Oh," he said. "It must be high as the Rocky Mountains."

They had taken a trip to Banff the year before, and the mountains had become his new measure of height.

"There's nothing that high in Scotland, but Arthur's Seat is pretty high."

"Oh," said Duncan.

"But the owl," Skye said, raising her voice and spreading her arms like giant wings. "There was a stray dog and a beautiful flock of cormorants but the owl, I'm sure, could have flown to the Rockies."

"Really?" said Duncan, dropping the tin man.

"Yes," said Skye. "At first we thought it was an eagle."

"Don't owls only fly at night?" asked Duncan, frowning, looking back down at his toy on the floor.

"This owl seemed to not care about the time of the day," she lied. "First there was her giant shadow, and then everything became gold as the moon. The owl dropped a grey feather into my lap, and I knew immediately why your grandfather had brought me to the hilltop."

"Why?" asked Duncan. "What did the feather tell you?"

"Well," said Skye. "As she flew closer, her eyes were big as gold saucers, and then as she came closer, they were small as peas. "

"Did it make any noises? Were there other people? Were you scared?"

"It made a large screeching noise. We were alone, but not frightened. I knew at that moment that your grandfather was a wise man. I also knew that he wanted to marry me, even before he brought out the ring."

"He asked you to marry him? Right there on top of the mountain? Did the owl carry the two of you away? Did it drop anything else in your lap?"

"The owl disappeared," said Skye. "But I knew," she said, taking Duncan's hand, "that I didn't ever want to be alone. Part of being smart is being with other people. Part of flying is touching down on the ground sometimes."

"Oh," said Duncan, picking up his car and making it fly. "No problem, Grandma Skye."

"You're thinking about your mom again, aren't you?" she asked.

"How did you know that?" he asked.

"The owl," said Skye, pulling a white feather out of her apron, "taught me to always trust my intuition."

"Intuition?"

"What you know inside," she said, tickling his ribs and belly. "What's in here and in here," she added, pointing to his heart and his head.

# KINCARDINE, 2011

Skye pulls her hair back and looks through blurred eyes at the clock above the stove. 5:16? Is that afternoon or morning? She could make herself a nice bowl of tomato soup and a cheese sandwich. Or is it porridge with a drizzle of maple syrup that she should be making? It's hard to tell in the winter when it seems to be dark morning and night. What time would that be in Edinburgh? she wonders.

•

When he was small, she'd say: "Not outside of the lines now, Duncan," and at first he would focus, try his best to please her and colour within the lines provided. Then he'd let himself go, scribbling over the drawing, covering every inch of the page. An orange house. A green pony. A purple butterfly.

"Houses are rarely purple in this country," she'd tell him. "Horses are grey or brown or black," she'd say, "not pink. And butterflies are never mauve."

Looking up at her with those brown eyes so full of trust and promise, he'd sit quietly and listen to her every word. She never had a problem with that boy. Her mother was wrong. Not all children needed to be *tamed*.

Duncan was well beyond colouring books and simple drawings; he'd be holed up in his room for hours at a time with an enormous pad of paper and his favourite charcoal pencils.

For his thirteenth birthday she bought him a copy of *Rendering in Pencil*. A large, beautiful book with illustrations and tips on drawing technique that spoke of the merits of the pencil as being cheap and accessible, with one of its greatest virtues being its *unusual freedom in correcting or erasing*. Skye liked the idea of being able to erase and start over. Duncan immediately sat down with the book in his lap, turning the pages, making tiny pencil notes in the margins. He quickly mastered the exercises and attempted to have her do the same.

"You can do it, Grandma Skye," he'd say. "Go with your imagination."

"My goodness," she said, "your drawings are better than the ones in the book."

She'd always seen herself as an illustrator, capable only of drawing cross-sectioned animals pre- and post-op, but what she really wanted was to draw home. She drew a castle on a treed hill, the Isle of Skye surrounded by the ocean. She teased out waves rolling against jagged rocks. Always easygoing and sensitive, Duncan was encouraging, a strong, natural teacher who was beyond his thirteen years.

"You want to draw the ocean," he said. "Then draw its power. Let the water crash onto the paper. Waves!" he'd say, laughing. "Press your fingers into the charcoal. Move your hand. Make big circles. Waves, Grandma! Not ripples."

Now Duncan is walking the halls of the Royal Dick, that solid stone building across from the Meadows that they now call Summerhall. Apparently, it was his friend, Siobhan, who convinced him to apply for a spot in the show.

If only she could reach him now. She'd shout out: *Paint Summerhall mauve if you like!*

Skye twists the ring on her finger. It annoys her when her ring is on the wrong hand, but she'll keep it there until she remembers. *What could it possibly be?* she mumbles. *That's it!* she shouts — *S. V. and R. R.*, carved into the wall when they were younger than Duncan is now; etched there, before the security guards came along. *You must see if our initials are still there.*

Skye is startled by the urgency in her voice. My goodness, she thinks. Is this what has become of her life — an old woman talking to herself at the kitchen table, shouting out across the ocean, reaching through waves of darkness? She pulls out the drawer under the table and removes the journal she's been keeping for years. She opens the front page and looks at her writing — it was strong then, large, rolling letters: *Life Lessons for Duncan*. She turns to the back of the book. Now, she can hardly read her own writing.

She picks up her pencil and writes — *Squirrel: Sciurus carolinensis:* followed by *Phylum: Chordata; Order: Rodentia; Family: Sciuridae.* She keeps things simple. *Description: pointed face, dark eyes.* She lifts her pencil and pauses, but keeps to her promise: *Attributes*, she writes — *None. They are persistent ….*

•

Skye lifts her head off the table. She has been crying in her sleep again, and she's smudged her drawing of the squirrel. The kitchen is dark and there's no light coming through the kitchen window; perhaps it is night time? And that noise? What is that scratching from behind the wall? If only she had the strength to pull out the stove. Could it be another squirrel gnawing through the chicken wire that Rory so diligently nailed in place all those years ago? Perhaps she can see between the cupboard and stove if she gets down on her knees. She'll face that critter eye to eye. This business will be finished with once and for all. But first she must eat. Skye pushes down on the table with both hands. It's difficult to stand, but slowly she manages to get to her feet. Porridge it is then, she thinks, turning to face the stove. Porridge is Duncan's favourite.

# PART III

# KINCARDINE, 1991

Skye loved Duncan more than anything in the world; there was never a natural inclination to love Moira and she felt terrible that everything had been a battle with her daughter. *It's natural to love what you give birth to,* her mother told her when Skye finally confided her despair over the telephone. Skye was shocked to hear these words from her mother and she didn't have to look too far to see that wasn't always true — even animals will sometimes turn away from their young.

*Do you think I could talk with Anne for a moment?* she asked her mother.

*Anne has gone back to her people,* her mother said. Skye thought she heard cheer in her voice, but then she realized that her mother was grief-stricken, holding back tears, pretending to have a raspy throat.

*How are you getting by without her then?* she asked, but her mother ignored her question.

*Love is complicated,* her mother said. *Love is different from person to person.* Skye changed the subject of the conversation to the weather and while her mother spoke about the constant drizzle over Edinburgh, she thought of Rory and how there was a comfort that came out of time that blossomed from year after year or sharing the same house and bed, but she wouldn't call it love. But Duncan, there was something about him that pulled at her from the moment she set eyes on him in Moira's arms — those brown eyes peering out from the blue blanket reached right into her and gripped her heart.

"Why do people say 'Elephants never forget'?" Duncan had asked her recently. It was a sunny April afternoon and they'd been having their first picnic of the year in the backyard of the Princes Street house.

"Because they don't," she told him.

"But how do you know?"

"I know because I've watched them in the zoo and on television. I've studied how they go back to the same watering hole. I've observed the way they recognize their young no matter how much mud and time between them. I've witnessed with my own eyes that they grieve the death of their young. They'll wait and wait, no matter how pointless, no matter what the evidence that their waiting is futile, their babies will never come back to life."

"Are you crying, Grandma?" he asked her.

"No, Duncan," she said, wiping her eyes.

"But the tears…?"

"Sorry, sweet boy," she said, rubbing her fingers through his head of dark curls. "Of course I'm crying. But I'm not sad," she added. "Sometimes people cry when they're happy too."

•

"Guess which animal?" Skye asked a few weeks later, the vacuum cleaner hose hanging from her nose, swaying from side to side.

"An anteater?" Duncan guessed.

"Nope," she said, raising the trunk with her arm and roaring.

"An elephant?"

"Nope," she said. "Guess again."

He looked her over. There was a snowstorm and there wasn't any electricity. The light that came into the playroom through the window was better than nothing, but it was late afternoon and beginning to get dark. The long tail made of a knotted bunch of his grandfather Rory's old ties looked like a donkey or horse's.

"A spirit?" he said.

"A spirit?"

"Yes," he said, proud of his imagination. "You look like the spirit of a hundred thousand dead animals."

"Well," Skye said. "That's quite an animal. But dead? Why are the hundred thousand animals dead?"

"Because that's your work. Thistle died."

"Thistle got hit by a car, Duncan. He died on the side of the road."

"Did it hurt?" he said, and, kicking at the floor with his bare foot, added, "I hate cars."

"It happened fast, sweet pea," she said, pulling him close, knowing perfectly well why he hated cars. "I would like to think she didn't suffer at all."

"I don't think we should let Rocky play outside anymore," he said.

Skye had found Rocky wandering the streets of Kincardine. She explained to Duncan that she was on her way home from the clinic one night, driving slowly because of the ice on the road. She could hardly make him out in the dark — mangy and missing teeth, his coat matted and dirty, growling as she approached.

"I don't know," she said, "He's an outside dog; let's ask him what he thinks. Rocky! Oh, Rocky, come here," she shouted.

Rocky came thumping into the room, wagging his tail, running to Duncan with kisses and then back to Skye. It was spring and there were scents in the air — newborn rabbits under the toolshed, the feral cat's litter of three.

"Mister Rocky," Skye asked. "Do you want to play outside in the sun today?"

Rocky ran out of the room and down the hallway. They could hear him barking at the front door.

"I don't think it would be so good to keep Rocky inside," she said. "But let's keep an eye on him."

"Hey, Grandma," Duncan asked. "What animal are you really?"

"A mastodon," she said.

"What's that?"

"An ancient creature from 40 million years ago. Like elephants, but different."

"That's not fair," Duncan said, kicking the fake trunk. "That's too hard for a nine-year-old kid."

"Well, you'll never learn if I don't challenge you a little," she said. "Now let's try a different animal," she continued, lying on the ground, slithering like a snake, her mouth wide open as if she were about to swallow a frog.

"You're weird," Duncan said. "I don't want to play anymore."

"Oh," she said, sitting up. "I guess these baggy old leg warmers don't look so great. There we go," she said, peeling off the grey wool from her arms and legs.

"Besides," he said, pointing to the door where Rocky stood with his leash hanging from his mouth. "Rocky wants to go for a *W-A-L-K.*"

# KINCARDINE, 1993

Skye held the bird in the cup of her hands. It was quiet and still. "Fly," she said, raising her arms and opening her hands. The bird fluttered to the roof of the house, made a small arc in the air, returned to her face-up palms. She stood perfectly still, turned her head slowly toward Duncan. "See," she said. "It always comes back. Animals know when to go and when to come back. And you're a boy who needs to get moving or else miss the school bus again."

Duncan didn't want to go to school. He didn't want to stand in front of the class and do a presentation about "What My Father Does for Work." He told the teacher he didn't know what his father did for work.

"Write about your grandmother then," she'd said.

Duncan hesitated. "My grandmother's a veterinarian."

"That's terrific, Duncan," she said, knowing perfectly well that his grandmother was a veterinarian. Everyone in town knew Skye Rayburn. "Perhaps you could tell us all a little bit more about what she does?"

"But I don't really know what she does with the animals."

"Ask her," his teacher said. "I'm sure she'd be more than happy to help you with your presentation."

Duncan didn't like his teacher. He didn't like the way she smelled like chalk and moth balls. He didn't like the tone of her voice when she spoke about Skye.

"Sure," he said, walking away.

"Duncan," his teacher called back. "Did I ever tell you that I was your mother's teacher as well?"

"No," he said, feeling sick to his stomach.

"She was a good girl, that Moira. Did everything she could to please her mother."

# KINCARDINE, 1994

Skye stood at the kitchen sink doing dishes, looking out at the tree next to the house; the tree where she'd found the nest after the squirrel had died.

Duncan was asking about Rory again.

"It's called pancreatic cancer," she said.

Duncan was twelve and moving quickly away from little-boy innocence. He wanted to know everything and was not easily tricked.

"When he was in the war, did he kill anyone?"

"It was World War Two, Duncan. I'm sure he did."

"Did you ever kill anything?" he asked, seemingly out of the blue.

Skye almost fell over.

"What did you say?"

"Like when someone brought an animal to see you and you couldn't fix it?"

"Well…yes," she said. "You know perfectly well that I see dying animals practically every working day."

"Does it make you sad when it happens?"

Skye took a minute, dug deep into the soapy water for the pot with the oatmeal caked onto the bottom.

"Sometimes I don't know the animal. Sometimes I don't feel anything."

"Will you be sad when Rocky dies?"

"Why, of course I'll be sad, Duncan. Don't be foolish."

"Were you sad when my father left?"

Skye didn't want to lie, but the truth wouldn't be helpful either. "I knew that you needed a father."

"Even a father like him?"

"Duncan," Skye said. "Your father had all kinds of good qualities."

"Like?"

"Like his strength. He was short, but all muscle."

"Was?" Duncan said.

"For the love of…" said Skye. "Is. I assume he still is short and strong. Now, no more questions today."

"Would you be sad if a squirrel died?" he asked.

She paused, but not too long.

"Duncan Johnson. Where are you getting these questions today? I don't know if *sad* is the right word," she said. "But I'd feel something, I imagine."

A few weeks earlier, she'd lectured him again about feeding a squirrel that he had coaxed into the house with peanut butter on crackers.

"I've told you about this before," she said. "Sometimes they have rabies, and sometimes they cause serious damage to a house if they get in.

"Like what?" he'd asked. "What kind of damage?"

"Chewing through electrical wires. Digging a hole in the attic so the rain gets in."

"Would you get revenge if it came into this house?" he asked.

Revenge? Where does he find these words? How does he always know what question she least wants him to ask?

"There's no such thing as revenge," Skye said, dropping the pot back in the water. "God always wins."

# KINCARDINE, 1995

"Phew," said Duncan. "It's a skunk."

"Skunks get hit a lot on the road," said Skye. "They don't see very well."

"Did my mom see very well?" asked Duncan.

"We've talked about this before," said Skye. "Your mom had perfect vision. Now let's see if we can find something on this cursed radio."

They were driving to Toronto. It was Duncan's thirteenth birthday and Skye was taking him to see the movie *Babe*.

"I'd rather see *Batman Forever*," said Duncan. "*Babe*'s for little kids."

"*Batman*'s too violent," said Skye.

"*Babe*'s too faggy," said Duncan.

"*Faggy*. Where do you learn language like that?" Skye asked, turning down the radio.

"School," said Duncan. "I told some of the kids at school I was going to see *Babe* and that's what they said."

"*Babe* is a good old-fashioned movie about a pig. You're going to like it."

"But can I tell them I saw *Batman*?"

Skye thought about it. More and more, Duncan seemed to be coming into an awareness about something. He would come home from school and lock himself in his room for hours. Sometimes he'd show her his sketchbook, sometimes not. Sometimes she peeked at what he'd drawn when he wasn't there.

"Tell them what you want," she said. "But I'm not going to encourage you to lie."

They drove for a long time with the radio off and the window open. They turned off Highway 9 and merged onto the 400.

"You lied," said Duncan, kicking off his shoes, pulling his knees into his chest.

"Oh?" said Skye, knowing perfectly well where the conversation was heading.

"Watch where you're driving," said Duncan. "Can't you hear the horns?"

"I hear the horns," Skye said. "They think I'm driving too slow. Don't you start telling me how to drive."

"You said it was ice on the road."

"It was ice on the road."

"What else?"

"It was ice on the road and snow."

"And booze."

"Who told you that?"

"Everyone knows, Skye. My dad's a drunk and he killed her."

Skye found it difficult to drive on the highway at the best of times. It had been years since Duncan had mentioned his father. This was not the conversation that she wanted to have as traffic grew thicker.

"I need to concentrate," she said.

"You always need to concentrate. I don't have to go to *Batman*. We can go to the pig movie."

"*Batman Forever* would be fine," she sighed, as the traffic slowed to a crawl.

•

Skye worried about Duncan. He was growing progressively silent and didn't seem to have friends. As far as she could tell, he didn't play ball or hang out after school with boys his age and he spent most evenings in his room sketching animals. She had suggested joining the school band, the swim team, and the debating club…but her suggestions only agitated him. Finally, one day as they sat sharing the last of the ice cream from the container, she had an idea.

"You're too old for Cubs," she said, licking chocolate off her fingers. "But as a Scout, you would make new friends."

"I don't think so," said Duncan. "But maybe I'll join 4-H."

"4-H?" Skye said. "It's mostly young girls in the Bruce County 4-H club. From what I know, they spend their time talking about cows, pigs and boys."

"That's okay," Duncan said, pausing with his spoon suspended above the ice cream. "I want to know more about...animals."

"Really?" said Skye. He was almost fourteen years old, and had never shown a great interest in her work.

"Well," said Skye. "I am on my way to help birth a sheep. Would you care to join me?"

"Sure," he said, dumping the empty ice cream container in the trash under the sink, "let's go."

●

A week earlier, the day before Father's Day, Duncan had been in Fincher's looking for a birthday card for his new friend, Siobhan. He walked up and down the aisles searching for something not too sentimental; maybe even one of those joke cards. Siobhan's birthday had just passed and she'd confided that she hadn't received a single card.

"Not even your parents?" he asked.

"They don't live together, and my dad's not on the scene."

Siobhan was two years younger than him, but to Duncan she was like an adult without the agenda. She didn't care what the other kids thought of her, and he liked the way she calmly walked in and out of trouble.

"Oh," said Duncan. "At least your mom's around."

"Whatever," she said. "The whole town calls her *Squirrely Shirley*. Sometimes I wish she wasn't. Wanna go down to the lake and smoke?"

As he passed the Father's Day rack, it occurred to Duncan that he had never had to buy a card for that particular occasion. He was curious. He walked to the Father, From Son section and picked up a brown and gold card with a set of gulf clubs on the cover:

*Who is a Father?*
*A father is always there for you…*

"Yeah, right," Duncan says to himself. He puts that card back in the rack and picks up the one next to it. There's a vintage car on the cover, a Rolls Royce.

*Dad, for all that you've done.*

Duncan starts to put the card back on the rack, but he misses the slot and it falls on the floor. It's just not fair. Lately he is confused about a whole pile of things — sex being on his mind all the time now. He has a million questions that he'd never ask Skye, or any girl for that matter. He's all messed up and he can't even put his thoughts into his drawings — they'd have men in them. They wouldn't be the kind of drawing he could show anyone. He didn't ask to be born. He is crying and worried that someone in the store will see him, but he can't stop himself. He didn't ask for a stupid runaway for a father. It's just not fair. He didn't ask to be dumped at his grandmother's without a single phone call, ever. Not one.

•

"You remember my grandson, Duncan?" Skye said to the grumpy farmer, who had walked into the sheep barn where the two of them were standing side by side. Duncan was almost as tall as Skye and she was proud of him when he extended his hand to the farmer to shake. And when the farmer turned away from Duncan, she felt like picking up her things and marching straight out of the barn.

"I thought I heard two girls in here," the farmer said.

"Just me and my fine assistant," Skye said. "As you know, I'm pretty much retired now and need a little help from time to time."

Duncan looked down. He kicked at some straw on the ground, aware that his face was turning red.

"He's at that age," said Skye. "Everything's changing, especially the voice."

But the farmer wasn't interested in male puberty; his concern seemed to be with his sheep.

"She's not doing well," he said to Skye, pointing to the ewe's abdomen. "She's been dropped for a while now."

The ewe's udder seemed full with colostrum, and Skye knew that the labour should have begun. She was glad that the ewe had been shorn; it was easier for her to see that the pelvic ligaments had loosened and that there was a hollow around the dock.

"She looks fat as a pregnant cow," Duncan said.

The farmer wasn't amused and didn't hide his feelings.

"Does he need to be here?" he asked, nodding at Duncan.

"He's here because I want him to be," said Skye. "Duncan," she said with exaggerated sternness, "she's big like this because she's late. She's having problems."

The ewe strained and pushed. Skye could see that she had passed her mucous plug and was weak. And as she debated whether or not to intervene, Skye noticed the sack protruding from the vulva and decided to let nature take its course. The ewe continued to grunt and strain.

"Stand closer," said Skye, placing one of Duncan's hands on the ewe's rump and the other on the emerging lamb. "Any second now."

When the ewe gave the final push and the lamb came shooting out, it sent Skye flying on her back. She had caught the lamb in mid-air, but wanted to set it down immediately — four legs, four eyes and ears — a two-headed lamb; one of the most sad and unusual creatures she had ever seen. It was breathing, the mucous-covered eye she looked down onto had blinked open and there was a faint bleating coming from its mouth.

But the lamb and ewe were the least of Skye's worries. Duncan had fainted and was passed out on the barn floor.

"You've got a problem on your hands," said the farmer looking at the lamb in her arms.

"More than you know," said Skye, placing the lamb in the straw and wiping her hands on her coat before lifting Duncan's head and placing it in her lap. "This isn't quite how I wanted his first experience to go."

# KINCARDINE, 1996

The Wilsons' toddler was missing and everyone in town had their own theory about what had happened. The newspaper said she'd been kidnapped because there was money in the family. Anyone who knew the family thought it was probably the mom. One day the doorbell rang and when Skye opened the door, there was a police officer with a very frightened look on his face.

"I'm Officer Frank Tester," he said. "Would you mind having a look over here, Doctor Rayburn?" motioning towards the cruiser.

"Give me a minute," she said, "while I get my robe."

"No problem," he said. "Take your time."

It was a cold January day; she could see his breath as he spoke, and he seemed to be shivering.

"Come in," she said.

Her bathrobe was thrown over the back of the sofa, so it only took a second, but he didn't seem in a hurry to get back out in the cold.

"Is anyone else at home?" he asked, flashing his identification. "We may need a witness."

"Witness to what," she said, squinting to read his badge, "Officer Tester?"

The officer continued to shake, and after a long, deep, breath, he said, "You know that Wilson kid that's missing?"

Skye put on her bathrobe and closed the door behind them. They walked over to the police car. The officer opened the trunk and pointed to three small boxes.

"We need to know if these are animal parts. We'll do this one first," he said. "I found it on the side of the road."

Skye looked into the box. It only took two seconds to figure out what she was looking at.

"It's a chunk of cow lung," she'd said. "It must have fallen off the dead stock truck."

"Oh," he said. "That's good. Are you sure?"

"Sure as sure can be," she said.

He reached into the trunk for the second box.

"They're bones," he said. "We found them in the woods. They have knife marks on them."

"Deer bones," she said, pointing to scars on the bones. "There are very few deer bones in the woods that don't have hunter's knife marks on them, or a bullet hole."

"Are you sure?" he asked, but her look gave him his answer before she could open her mouth.

"Okay," he said. "Two down, one to go."

He pulled out the third box. It was longer and wider than the first two. He paused before opening the lid. "It's strange what some people will do," he said. "We found his skeleton down by the pier."

Over the years, there'd been plenty of bones found down by the pier. The train station and cattle yard used to be there, before they put in the parking lot. Skye thought that she'd have a little fun with the officer.

"If you're so sure it's the Wilson child," Skye said, starting to shiver because of the cold, "why aren't you bringing his remains to the coroner's house on a Sunday morning?"

The officer took his time with his answer. He looked down at the box, then up at her. "I don't want to look like a fool if it's not him," he said.

"It's all there," she said. "Side section of skull, leg bone, the hip…"

"Oh, oh," said the officer, already reaching his hand in the window for the car phone.

"But wait," Skye said. "This skull…how old was the boy?"

The officer had put down the receiver. "Two," he said.

"This piece of skull's a little large, could be an adult male."

"Adult?" said the officer, pulling his coat closer, standing next to her as she held up the skull for a better look.

"Put that thing down," he said. "We don't want the whole world to know."

Skye placed the skull fragment in the box, exaggerating her emotions. "Go gently," she said. "Rest in peace, my sorry little four-legged creature."

"*Four-legged creature* — are you yanking my chain?" the officer said. "Skye Rayburn, I've heard about you."

"Really?" Skye smiled.

"They say that you're a jokester."

"And who are *they*?" she asked.

"Never mind," he said, pointing to the pile of bones. "Is this or isn't this the Wilson kid?"

"It's a calf skeleton," she said. "There used to be a stockyard down there years ago."

"Thank you for your time this morning." He slammed the car door.

"My pleasure, Officer Tester," she called, as snow drifted over her fuzzy pink slippers and the wind blew open her robe.

•

A few weeks later when Skye opened her front door and Officer Tester was there, he was not alone.

"Doctor Rayburn," he said. "Is this one yours?"

Everyone in town knew that Duncan was her grandson. Most people knew that she was his guardian and that he lived with her.

"Yes," she said. "Step in."

"You seem a little more concerned about neighbours today than the last time we met," he said, smirking.

Duncan stood with his head down. His hair was long and he looked like every other teenager in Kincardine with his jean jacket and torn jeans.

"What in God's name has happened?"

Duncan remained silent with his head down.

"There's nothing on the floor for you to stare at, Duncan," she said. "Now please look up and tell me what's going on."

"It seems that your boy likes his marijuana," said Officer Tester, nodding over his shoulder to the police cruiser parked in front of the house.

"We found him and the girl smoking down by the water filtration plant."

Skye could see Siobhan in the back seat of the cruiser. Even from twenty metres, she could see the scowl on her teenage face. She didn't look so much like her mother anymore. Skye couldn't put her finger on it, but Siobhan, at a distance, reminded her of someone else she knew.

"And before you say anything," said the officer, holding up a small baggie of marijuana, "we found this tucked inside his boot."

"Duncan?" she said. "Please tell me you're not on the same downward path as your father."

•

"Uphill. Growing up in Edinburgh seemed to be climbing rocks and rolling down mossy hills. And the sea — there's plenty of water in Scotland, I tell you."

More and more, now that he was older, Duncan was interested in learning about where she was from.

"That's it?" he said. "Hills and water? Don't you have stories about the people where you lived? Didn't you have dates or anything before you met Grandpa Rory?"

"Don't be precocious," Skye said. "There was a war going on."

"Thought you said your parents had tons of money."

"They did have money," she said. "But their money didn't buy me adventure."

"I don't see how that's possible," Duncan said, bending over to tie up his shoelace. "Rich people can get whatever they want."

"Boy, have you got things to learn there," she smiled, ruffling his hair.

He didn't want to go to his practice game. Skye had signed him up for baseball, and she wanted him to stop dragging his heels. She didn't have a clue how to raise a boy; God knows she didn't get it right with Moira. Rory, on the other hand, always knew what to say. When her period came, Skye had seen Moira hiding something white and slender up the sleeve of her sweater as she tippy-toed past them on her way out the door for school.

"Is that a cigarette?" Skye blurted out.

"Mother," she said, turning red. "No…"

"Oh," she'd said, when Moira tried to discreetly show her the tampon without Rory seeing. "Your period," she blurted out.

"Hey there, my little Sunflower," Rory said, easing the conversation, as he always did. "It's just part of growing into a woman."

Moira smiled at him, but gave Skye a dirty look as she marched out the door.

Duncan switched legs and tied the other shoelace. He was fourteen and attractive.

"You know you look just like him," Skye said.

"Him?"

"Yes," said Skye, already feeling that she'd be stepping into something she shouldn't. "Your father."

"And did you know that Dolly was created from a boob?"

"Watch your mouth, Duncan," she said. "I'm being serious, your dad was a good-looking man."

"That's your problem," he said. "You're always serious."

"Really?" she said. Duncan wasn't a hurtful kid, and she took what he said to heart.

"Well, sort of," said Duncan, softening his voice. "Sometimes. Anyhow, Dolly, the clone sheep, was made from a mammary gland, so they named her after the original Big Boob country singer, Dolly Parton."

"That's not so," said Skye, feeling her face flush. "Where did you get that from?"

"Jeez, Grandma Skye," he said. "For a veterinarian you're pretty uptight about nature."

"I'm not so sure that's nature," she said. "This cloning stuff."

"Well, boobs are," he said.

She didn't know what to say, but she figured she had to try. More and more Duncan had been weaving sex into their conversations. She inhaled, reassured herself that there was no need to worry, Duncan was an open-minded, good-natured kid. Besides, maybe this time she'd get it right.

"Duncan," she said. "Sit down for a moment. The reason I mentioned your father…"

He took a seat, folded his arms, tilted his head to one side. "Yes?" he said.

Skye cleared her throat, pulled up a chair beside him and sat tall. "Well," she said. "Normally the dad would have this conversation with his son, but given the circumstances…"

She held her hands together, as if she were praying, but immediately realized how pious that would look to a teenager. She moved her wedding ring from one hand to the other, made a note to look up that old Kinsey Report that she'd kept on her bookshelf all these years. She relaxed her shoulders, leaned back in her chair, tried to act casual.

"Are you being, urgh, hum, intimate, with any girls right now?"

"Gross," Duncan said, pushing back his chair and standing. "This is really gross," he said, running out the door, tossing the baseball bat from one hand to the other as he ran down the street.

Well, that went off well, she chuckled at her failed attempt at fatherhood. She wanted him to know that sex was more than passion. She wanted him to know that the immediacy of aroused flesh and kissing and the prying and the pounding and the promises…can all result in something more permanent. She wanted him to know that more than one person gets hurt when things go awry, and that there are consequences to letting one's body rule over one's head.

•

His grandfather had died before he was born, but Duncan had heard the story about how Rory and Skye had met in Scotland.

"You must go there some day," Skye told him. "Edinburgh is famous for its cliffs and castles, but it's also famous for its big festival."

"Where did you live?" he asked her.

"In the city," she said. "It was smaller back then."

"Did you like it?" he asked.

"I love Scotland," she said.

"Why did so many people leave Scotland?"

Skye knew why she'd left, but wasn't so sure about the others.

"I suppose they came to Canada for a better life," she answered.

"Is that why you came here?" he asked.

"I suppose," she said. "But not exactly."

"Then why didn't you go back?"

Skye set down the tea towel and sat at the table next to Duncan. At first she didn't want to, but as the years passed and she started to get older, she felt a deep longing to go back to Scotland.

"I've been waiting, I guess."

"Waiting?"

"Yes, sweet boy," she said. "I always figured that your father would come back to this house."

From time to time Duncan tried to imagine his father. Skye told him that she always thought of Magnus as a kind-hearted man, although somewhat lost. She said he was short and wiry, very handsome. Duncan wondered what it would be like to have a father shorter than himself — he'd hit the six-foot mark in grade nine.

"But didn't your mom and dad miss you?"

"I suppose," said Skye, not so sure of the truth of her words. "My father would have missed me for sure."

"And my father," Duncan asked. "Do you think that jerk even knows I'm alive?"

•

Officer Tester left Duncan with Skye. Once the door was closed, she turned to him and made him promise to never smoke marijuana again.

"But it wasn't me, I tell you. I don't like pot."

"You've tried it then?" she said.

"Once. After school."

"With her, I suppose?"

"Yes," he said, looking down at the floor.

Duncan didn't want to rat on Siobhan, but he also didn't feel it did either of them any good to lie to Skye — she always knew when he wasn't telling the truth.

"We have a deal," he said. "Remember? We promised to always tell each other the truth no matter what. I'm not lying."

"Okay," said Skye. "I believe you. What in God's name do you see in that girl?"

In school, even though he was the tallest, Duncan was the last one chosen for any team sport and he didn't know how to talk with boys his age. It was easier to hide in the library and draw or, some days, not to go to school at all. With Siobhan it was easy. He saw that she was the same — doodling in the margins of her text book, always alone. One day she'd come to school with purple hair; another day with blue or red. She spoke out against the Conservative government in social studies class, and was constantly disciplined for inappropriate clothing or shocking language.

"She's not a bad person," he said. "She's just expressive."

"That may or may not be true, Duncan, but she's destined for trouble."

# KINCARDINE, 1997

"Thank God I'm not alone," Siobhan told him.

"What are you talking about?" he said, looking puzzled.

"You're gay, aren't you?" she asked.

She watched him turn red. She watched him turn away and kick at the snow.

"*Maybe*," she thought she'd heard him say under his breath. Maybe she crossed a line. People have told her she's too pushy. She should have waited for him to tell her.

They were standing by the wall at the water filtration plant. They'd attempted a walk down by the lake, but it was too cold.

"Just stand with me while I have a smoke," she said. "Don't worry about the gay thing."

"It'll freak my grandmother out," he said.

"She's already a freak," Siobhan said.

"That's not very nice," Duncan told her, kicking at the snow until he reached the pavement.

"I'm just kidding. I like Skye," she said, inhaling her cigarette. "Hey, Duncan," she asked, exhaling, "do you ever think of your dad?"

Duncan didn't answer at first. He reached out and took her cigarette and inhaled deeply.

"Hey, you don't smoke, you goofball," she'd said.

"Don't think of him much," he lied, coughing out smoke. "I hardly ever think of that jerk. But sometimes I wonder what it would be like to have a regular mom instead of Skye."

•

At the edge of the forest, between daytime and night, a fox appeared like a flash of gold in the late summer trees.

"Heel," Skye said to Rocky.

Rocky had been sniffing around the ground where they were walking. He must have picked up the scent of the fox or some other animal that had been on the path earlier. Together they sat near a fallen tree.

"I need to be still today, Rocky," she said.

He looked up when he heard his name.

"The Princess of Wales has died and I'm a little in shock."

The world was once more peaceful, the domain of animals who wandered free. They were worshipped by shamans, and envied by the gods. Then they were captured — slaughtered for food and fur by some; pampered and beautified by others as pets. This was what she loved best about Canada — the places where deer, bear and fox still wandered the forests.

The fox rolled in the sun-bleached grass. There seemed to be an unspoken pact to keep a safe distance. As Skye calmed herself and pondered the accidents that killed Moira and Diana, the fox trotted into the woods, its bushy tail level with the horizon, the sun rolled behind the last clouds of August and the trees seemed to sigh as a significant breeze pushed through them.

"Curse the inventor of cars," she said to Rocky, who pressed himself into her leg as she scratched behind his ear. "Were neither of those gallivanting women aware that they had young children to live for?"

# KINCARDINE, 1998

"Is she your girlfriend?" Skye asked, as she pulled down on the knot she had just made in his tie.

"Not really," Duncan said, looking down at his shoes. "Do we have any black shoe polish?"

"No," she said. "Stop being evasive."

"Well, she isn't," said Duncan, raising his voice. "You know she's not my girlfriend."

"Whoa," said Skye. "It's just a question."

"Do you have twenty dollars?" he snapped.

"You get more bees with honey," she said.

"What's that supposed to mean?"

"It means say *please*," she said, picking her purse off the kitchen table. "Love is complicated," she added.

"Love!" he shouted. "What are you talking about?"

"I'm saying if you have a date with a girl you need to respect her."

"It's just the Sunset Grill for my *friend's* birthday."

"And let me tell you that a girl's fourteenth birthday is a big deal."

"I know that," said Duncan, taking a twenty-dollar bill from her hand. "Why are you lecturing me?"

"You should pay for her too," she said, looking at the bill in his hand.

"I have twenty-five of my own," he said. "From work."

Duncan worked at McDonald's two shifts a week. At first she was worried that other teenagers would drop by and tease him. But, after a few weeks of stumbling through his shyness and giving too much change to customers, he blossomed in ways she couldn't have imagined.

"Perfect," she said, winking. "The lucky girl gets dessert too."

"Grandma Skye," he said. "Don't get your hopes up."

She felt those words like a punch in her chest. Of course he was *gay*, as they liked to say these days, but how could that be? His father was a womanizer and Rory couldn't get enough of her. She knew something about homosexuals from Graeme and Big Red. But still, she wondered how these things came about, seemingly out of nowhere. Then again, even with the animals she'd worked with over the years — two male dogs humping one another; the stud that she watched mount the gelding who seemed indifferent about the ordeal, chewing oats from a bucket while the other horse worked itself into a lather; two female cats together for life, one of them starving herself to death after the first one died.

"What are you saying, Duncan?" she asked.

"Nothing," he said, taking the tie off and dropping it on the chair where her purse was. "People don't wear ties out anymore."

"Does she have a name?"

"Siobhan," he said. "Siobhan Kellins. My friend. You know who she is."

"The Irish one?" said Skye.

"I guess she's Irish. I never asked," said Duncan kissing her on the cheek. "See you around eleven."

Skye kissed him back. "Siobhan Kellins," she said, as the screen door slammed and the double realization sunk into her chest.

•

A few weeks later, Duncan came home from his shift at McDonald's and announced that he had spoken to the guidance counsellor at his school. He said that she was invited to a family session, and he handed her a sheet of paper that read: PFLAG, with a phone number on it.

"What, for the love of Pete, is PFLAG?" she'd asked him, even though she'd already figured it out. "What did you do to your brand new denim jacket?" she yelled, looking at the rainbow flag patch he had sewn on to the shoulder.

"Parents and Friends of …"

"Oh I know, for crying out loud," she said. "I just didn't know what else to say."

Skye thought about calling Graeme, but he was old and from the *caveman times,* as Duncan would say. There must be some male figure in town that he could talk to. Who was this guidance counsellor? What if it's a phase? What if he runs off to Toronto and gets AIDS?

"No, I'm not going to get AIDS. And, no, I'm not running away to Toronto," he said, as if he'd read her mind. "I like this place."

"I know that you're not that irresponsible."

"I'm just telling you because the counsellor said it's always best to be honest with your parents. And you are my parents," he said.

"So I am," she said, handing him back the paper. "We can talk about this tomorrow. I'm off to Bervie to see a sick cow."

•

The cow was down in a snowbank and the prolapsed uterus was the size of a kitchen table. She'd lost a lot of blood and Skye knew that repositioning the uterus was going to be tough. The smell of dung mixed with blood was strong, almost overwhelming, and the farmer was no help. He nodded his head in the direction of the cow in the blood-soaked slush, said: "I was expecting a man vet."

She tied one end of a rope around the cow's neck and another to the fence post. There were icicles forming around her nose. The farmer turned and walked back toward the barn, where a boy stood alone. After a minute, the boy came and stood between her and the cow. He was twelve or thirteen, and was shivering when he mumbled with his head down: *I have to help.* The snow started to fall again and the wind stirred up the snow. Skye put her hand on the cow's heaving belly, and talked to her as she worked. She was talking to the cow, but was also talking to the boy, who seemed terrified.

"This won't be so bad," she said. "Go find us a plank."

"A plank?" he said, hardly able to speak.

"Yes," said Skye. "A piece of wood. And hurry, this cow is about to bleed to death and my hands are turning to ice."

Steam coming off the cow and blood splattering the snow around her, Skye lifted the uterus, which must have weighed forty pounds. The cow moaned and tried to stand, but her legs had no strength and she dug herself into a snow and mud hollow.

The boy came back, panting in the cold. He had something that looked like an old ironing board.

"I found this in the barn," he said.

"Slip it under," Skye instructed. "Hurry," she said, turning back to the cow.

She couldn't see the boy's face, but she could see him sliding in the muddy snow. She talked to the cow's heaving belly.

"These things happen sometimes," she said. "Sometimes a cow makes one push too many and the whole kit-and-caboodle comes out. What's her name?"

Skye's arms were burning from the weight of the work. She slid her hand inside the cow and pushed a few more inches. The boy didn't answer her question, so she repeated it.

"What do you call her? " Skye said.

"We're not allowed to give them names," the boy said.

"Of course you are; every farm animal should have a name. Lift the board," she told the boy. "Lift the board and angle it down."

The boy tried to lift, but fell back in the snow.

"I had a pig once," he said. "I didn't tell anyone, but I called her Penelope."

"Penelope!" Skye laughed, sliding in the mud.

"Yes," said the boy. "Then we had to kill her for food."

"Oh," said Skye.

"Don't get too attached, my father says. No names. No favourite animals at this farm."

"Lift," said Skye. "On the count of three — one, two, three, lift!"

Skye punched in a few more inches and was beginning to make progress when the cow moaned and pushed back. She slid into the slush of the bloody snow and the boy fell with her. From the corner of her eye she could see the farmer standing at a distance. It was a test that she would not fail. The boy was older than Duncan. What will this boy be when he becomes a man, she wondered? Will he stay on his father's farm or head off to the city to work in a factory or department store? Where is his mother? These were questions she would likely never know the answer to. Even after all these years, Skye still had a long way to go before some of the Bruce County farmers would trust her. The older men were private at the best of times, and they shut down when they saw that a woman was about to perform a task that seemed pretty straightforward, something they ought to be able to do without paying for help. *Just shove the whole darn thing back in*, one farmer said to her. *I'd do it for myself except birthing is girl business.*

"It's natural," Skye told the boy, reaching out her hand to help him up.

He wouldn't take her blood-covered hand, and she understood. Blood was familiar to her. Blood for a veterinarian is neither good nor bad — it's part of what forms a living, breathing creature.

She faced the cow, and pulled back on her hind legs. "Okay, Missy," she said. "We're going to do this whether you like it or not."

Skye looked over her shoulder for the farmer, but he had disappeared. The boy had propped up the board. Together they heaved: *One. Two. Three. Lift.*

It will all work out in the end. Her thoughts had shifted to Duncan and Magnus for some reason. It will all work out, she thought as the farmer came back to the barn with two cups of steaming chocolate — miracles happen every day.

# KINCARDINE, 1999

"**D**on't you think it's weird about your father?" Siobhan asked, taking a long drag off her cigarette. It was a few weeks from their graduation and they were hanging out in their usual place, the water filtration plant, down by the lake. They were killing time before the banquet — Duncan was getting an award from his school for his drawing of a beaver that had been selected to be on a new, limited-edition Canadian stamp.

"What do you mean *weird*?" Duncan said. "And do you have to blow smoke in my face every time you take a drag?"

"Oops, sorry," she said, turning her head to the side to exhale. "You know. Like he just took off like that."

"I guess," he said.

"Is it strange not having a dad around?"

"Can we talk about something else, Siobhan? I don't know why you always have to get into this stuff about my dad. He left. He's gone. He could be dead, for all I know."

Siobhan was his *beard*. It was a term she learned in gender studies class for women who are covers for gay men at social events in order for them to pass as heterosexual. He didn't like the term; she was his friend, plain and simple, he tells her time after time. And this father thing, he didn't understand her obsession.

"What about your father?" he asked. "I mean, like, you never say anything about him."

"There's not much to say. He and my mom are sort of non-entities — they were together and now they're not, no big deal," she insisted, butting out her cigarette against the wall.

"Oh," said Duncan, scratching his head. "Sort of like my dad."

"Sort of," said Siobhan. "Only I'm 99.999% sure that *my* dad's not dead."

•

Duncan slammed down the receiver but didn't say a word. Skye and Siobhan looked at one another, but remained silent. The telephone rang again, and Duncan shook his head.

"I'm not answering it," he said, folding another orange flyer, tossing it onto the pile.

"What happened?" asked Skye. "Duncan, what happened on that last call?"

"They said he was a one-trick pony," said Duncan, looking down at the table. "They said flash-in-the-pan Jack's pity party for homeless drunks won't get him elected."

"What do they know," said Siobhan. "Remember…no hang-ups about…"

"They said, if I want to find my father, that I should look in the drunk tanks on Spadina, but to not make an entire campaign of it."

•

It was about two weeks before the three of them worked together on the Jack Layton campaign. Skye had the photograph of his mother and father in front of her on the kitchen table. Duncan saw the softness in her eyes and heard the hurt when she spoke, but he couldn't stop himself.

"He was the one who left!" he yelled. "I was just a kid."

"Well, you're not a kid now," she said.

Duncan had thought about his dad on and off for most of his life. He'd wondered what it would have been like to be a more normal family. He saw the dads picking up other kids at school. He saw the dads holding hands with their sons and daughters at the Saturday night bagpipe parade down the main street. Then he would think about his mother and get angry.

"He killed her!" Duncan shouted again.

"There's always two sides to a story," Skye told him. "And lower your voice."

She left the photo on the table in front of him and moved to the sink, where she stood peeling onions for lasagne. It was his birthday, and he had made a special request.

"Two sides to a story!" he yelled. "She was your daughter. How could you even say that?"

Skye dropped the onion in the sink and rubbed her eyes with her sleeve. The burning was uncomfortable and she wanted to splash cool water in them, but her rage overruled.

"Don't you yell at me, young man," she said. "I'm well aware that Moira was my daughter."

"Well, it sounds like you're taking his side," said Duncan, lowering his voice.

"I'm not," she said, rubbing her eyes. "Trust me, I am not taking your father's side over your mother's. You see, Duncan. She's gone. Your mother's gone, but your father isn't. There's time."

"For what?" he said.

"To make amends."

"Amends? There's no excuse for what he's done."

"Perhaps," said Skye. "But you have to have that conversation."

•

"The mouth and esophagus don't always control how big the stomach is," Skye said.

"What is she talking about?" asked Siobhan.

They were having the all-you-can-eat buffet at Mandarin Restaurant.

"She's saying your eyes are bigger than your stomach."

"Do you two always have to talk in riddles and metaphors?" Siobhan asked.

"All right," said Skye. "A boa constrictor has a mouth that unhinges, so that it can swallow a calf. That's a horrifying image for the observer, but no big surprise if you know about snakes."

"Yes?" asked Siobhan.

"She's saying guilt is a wasted emotion," said Duncan.

"There are people in this world who are starving to death as we gorge," Skye said.

"My God!" laughed Siobhan. "All that because I'm leaving food on my plate. Your grandmother is too weird for this planet."

# KINCARDINE, 2011

Skye stands at the stove and reaches to the back burner for her porridge pot. It's a small cast-iron pot that has seen better days, but is perfectly fine for porridge. Curse him, she thinks. Curse Magnus Johnson and his worthless guilt.

She carries the pot over to the sink and fills it with warm water. She carries it back to the stove, spilling along the way.

Throwing himself into the lake would have been easier, anything more efficient than thirty years of alcohol. A gun would have done the trick too, or the right combination of pills, but to drag this thing out just isn't right.

She turns the burner on high and uses her walker to manoeuvre around to face the table, *Slow, Skye Rayburn, inch your way back. Slow.*

# PART IV

# EDINBURGH, 2011

Broughton Street was easy to find on the map, and once he got closer he knew he was in the right neighbourhood by the rainbow flags hanging over the entrances of a few of the pubs. The guide said that the Blue Moon was a *good old-fashioned café* with decent food and large portions, but when Duncan walked in he wanted to turn right around. The place was dark and felt more like a tired bar than a café, but a good-looking guy in a tight black T-shirt caught his eye.

"Table for one, please," he told a waiter who stepped out from behind the bar reeking of cheap cologne, looking like he'd partied all night.

"How's this?" he asked Duncan, placing the menu down on an empty table next to the man with the black T-shirt.

The man smiled and Duncan looked away. He had never been great at talking to strangers. *That's why you're still single at twenty-nine*, Siobhan constantly told him. *You're practically an old maid.*

He sat with his back to the man, facing the bar. The art on the walls wasn't very good — most of his grade eleven students could do better.

Duncan lifted his backpack off the floor where he'd placed it close to the wall. He pulled out his sketch pad, glasses, and the Summerhall Festival Programme. He wanted to meet the man in the black T-shirt, but wasn't sure how to go about it. He thought about different excuses to strike up a conversation. The weather? The menu? Directions? Finally, he swung around in his chair.

"Do you know where this place is?" Duncan asked, his heart racing as he pointed to the Summerhall Festival Programme.

"Pardon?" said the guy in the black T-shirt, who was on his cellphone.

"Oops. Sorry," Duncan said. "I didn't realize…"

"Have the banoffee pie for dessert."

"Oh," said Duncan, turning to face him. He looked to be about thirty. His hair, cut short and spiky, was perfectly white, making his blue eyes stand out.

"What's banoffee pie?"

"It's a sickeningly delicious pastry with bananas, cream, toffee…the tourists go wild for it. You're from the States, right?"

"Canada. A small town, near Toronto."

"Oops, that's a faux pas. I hear that Canadians hate being called American."

"Hate's a strong word," said Duncan. "Besides, we like the U. S. again now that Obama's in."

"I'm Paul," the guy said, standing next to Duncan's table. He was solid and slick like a cop, only too short to really be on the police force — but hot, hot and sexy.

"I'm Duncan," he said, hardly able to get the words out of his mouth.

"Are you going to Summerhall?" he asked, nodding at the Festival Programme on the table.

"I have a show there," Duncan blurted out.

"You're kidding," said Paul, pulling up a chair. "Do you mind?"

"No problem."

"I like your shirt," said Paul.

Duncan's orange T-shirt said *PARTY ANIMAL* across the chest.

"Thanks," he said. "My friend Siobhan gave it to me when we were working on a campaign together. I'm really not a party animal, I'm actually pretty introverted."

The waiter brought a half-empty cup of coffee and half-eaten piece of pie from the table where Paul had been sitting and asked Duncan if he were going to have dessert.

"Yes," he said. "That banana cream thing sounds good."

When the waiter left the table, Paul moved his chair closer to Duncan and reached across for the Summerhall Programme.

"What's the name of your play?" he asked.

"Are you ready for this?" Duncan said. "It's called 'I was raised by a pack of wild wolves.'"

"That sounds like quite a show. What night is it on?"

"It's not a play," said Duncan. "I'm on page fifteen. I'm an artist. It's an exhibition of my drawings."

"This one's terrific," said Paul.

The drawing he'd pointed to was of Rocky rolling in snow.

"That's our dog, Rocky, who died."

"Do you have pets other than Rocky?" Paul asked. Duncan felt their knees brush under the table.

"No other pets," Duncan said. "But I live with my ninety-one-year-old grandmother, who was a veterinarian."

"Ninety-one?" said Paul.

"Yep. Alive and kicking as we speak."

"I'm a playwright," said Paul, flipping the pages of the Summerhall Programme. "I'm page twenty-one."

"You are indeed," laughed Duncan. There was a photo of Paul, centre stage and naked. A line of nude actors, male and female, stood behind him.

"It's the first time I've written and acted. It's called *Motion*. It's about movement, photography and the body. So ..." said Paul, the pressure from his knee becoming more intentional, "in answer to your earlier question, I know exactly where Summerhall is."

"Actually," said Duncan, smiling, "I do too. I was just..." He felt his face flush as he turned away from Paul. "I'm staying at the Roxburghe."

"I can walk you there."

"Thanks, but no," said Duncan. "I'm meeting my friend Siobhan in a few minutes."

"Oops," said Paul. "You're a shy Canadian."

"There's a Priape store in Toronto," Duncan said, nodding at a black bag next to the chair where Paul had been sitting. Aware that

Priape sold clothing and cards and was also known for its selection of gay pornography, Duncan knew he was bringing the conversation into a different level.

"And Montreal," said Paul, picking up the bag and pulling out what looked like a porn magazine. "I use the illustrations for inspiration."

"You've been to Montreal?" asked Duncan, leafing through the book.

"When I was a teenager," said Paul. "My father was presenting a paper at McGill."

"Your father's a professor?"

"My mother as well," said Paul, rolling his eyes and making a grand gesture like a king on his throne. "He's Lord Byron and she's Dante."

"That's quite a lineage," said Duncan. "Do you have any siblings?"

"A brother and a sister," said Paul. "We are the perfect family — two point five children and a dog."

"Who gets to be the .5?"

"Guess?" Paul said. "My *brilliant* parents couldn't cope with having a queer son. How 'bout you?"

"It's just me and my grandmother," he said, picking at the pastry on his pie. "She's from here. Her name is Skye."

"And your mum and dad?"

"It's a long story. My mom's dead and my dad just kind of disappeared. It was kind of lonely."

"Oh," said Paul.

"Are your grandparents alive?" Duncan asked, wanting to move the conversation away from his mother and father.

"My grandparents on my mom's side are pretty old and Grandma Francesangeli is dead."

"Your grandmother was Italian?"

"My mother's name is Giovanna," Paul said. "Giovanna Francesangeli-MacDougall, the Queen of Dante."

"Wow!" laughed Duncan. "I love it."

"By the way," said Paul. "You don't have to be an only child to be lonely."

Duncan felt the sincerity in Paul's words; felt as though he were talking to someone he could trust.

"Maybe we can go to Harry's Seat tomorrow or something? Skye says that's where she went on her first date with my grandfather."

Paul seemed to be trying to suppress a laugh by sipping his coffee.

"Arthur's Seat," he finally blurted out. "I would be happy to show you Arthur's Seat if you want, tomorrow. But first, are you going to the Summerhall pre-opening party tonight at the Dissection Room bar?"

"Yes," Duncan said. "I'd planned on going with my friend, Siobhan."

"See you there?" said Paul, standing to leave.

"See you there," said Duncan, wanting to pull him back, kiss him, run through the streets shouting *YES! YES! YES!*

•

The spirit of a hundred thousand dead animals looks like a prehistoric elephant and smells like lavender and formaldehyde. Black as a crow, her tusks are as long as a horse's ribs, and she sways from side to side like a snake. Her eyes are a lidless maze of blue vessels and tiny red veins, and her jaw is a weave of fat and muscle. She opens her mouth and a roar — not an old woman's whisper — comes out. In the dark, above the bartender, the vague outline of the mastodon head begins to form, followed by the feeling of her. Skye, as the embodiment of every animal she'd ever cured or euthanized.

Duncan steps away from Paul. He holds onto the iron railing, debates whether or not to climb the winding staircase to the upper level of the Dissection Room bar. He feels dizzy and might be sick. Why here? What could possibly bring a feeling of Skye so strongly into the room? It's just after 11:00 p.m.; that would make it early evening at home. Maybe she's fallen? Maybe Cathy has forgotten to check in on her? Maybe she's all right and is having a bowl of tomato soup and a grilled cheese sandwich, her favourite. She'll likely be looking for Rocky again, calling up and down the street for a dog that has been dead for years. *Princes Street, not Princess. The same as in Edinburgh*, she used to say. He should never have left Kincardine — *Rocky, get home here this minute* — Skye's probably leaning on her walker, shouting from the door off the kitchen; confused about what day it is, placing an X on her calendar, twice in one day.

"Are you all right?" asks Paul, standing close, placing his hand on Duncan's shoulder.

"I feel kind of sick," Duncan says. "Do you know where the washrooms are?"

Duncan leaves Paul standing at the bar and staggers through the room. He pushes toward the light of the washroom, past the glass cabinets with their cross-section posters of camels, horses and cows. Past leather sofas and wingback chairs set up like a well-appointed den and a print of a blue pig hung on the wall and a black cat and a pink cat. Past the jawbones and teeth of a bulldog. He feels her weight and heavy breathing, in and out against his side, guiding him as he navigates the dark. It's Skye. He's 100% sure that it's her. He knows her heart and that strength. He'd recognize her insistent nudge anywhere.

There are lockers and broken-down sinks, cubicles but no urinals. All of the stalls have tinted windows and some of the doors are missing altogether. The room is spinning and he'd do anything to stop the pounding behind his eyes. August at home often means humidity and heat which brings on headaches, but it is cool and rainy in Edinburgh. He feels sick to his stomach and wonders if he has food poisoning.

Duncan kneels next to the toilet but isn't able to vomit. He feels a slight contraction in his stomach, but nothing comes up. Then he hears someone enter the stall, sees a pair of familiar red running shoes.

"Siobhan, is that you?" he asks, without lifting his head from the toilet. "What are you doing in here?"

"What are *you* doing in here?" she says back. "Are you sick?"

Then it comes in a rush. Tightening and dizziness and finally the vomit flows. Duncan grips the toilet seat until he feels the final contraction.

"Phew," he says to Siobhan, who has entered the stall. "That was bad."

Siobhan gently rubs between his shoulders. "Have you been drinking?" she asks.

"One lousy Scotch," he says, trying to stand. He leans on the toilet tank to steady himself and the top comes loose. He almost falls over, but catches himself. He stands and fidgets with the lid trying to fit it back on when he notices a heart with initials curved into the wall. He leans in for a closer look:

*S . V. + R. R.*

"Are you all right?" Siobhan asks, handing him a handful of tissue.

"This is too weird," he says, ignoring Siobhan's question. "These are my grandparents' exact initials — Skye Vannan and Rory Rayburn."

"**R**ight here?" Skye asked Rory. "In the cloakroom?"

These days it would be called a unisex, but back then, it was the room where the veterinary students went to scrub up before and after surgery or to use the toilet. Each student had her own locker and some of them kept coats or shawls in them for the all-night study sessions in the cold, damp building.

"We could just stretch out together," Rory had assured her, pouring more Scotch from his flask into her paper cup. "We can keep our clothes on."

"But what if," she started to say as he propped a chair against the door, "someone comes in."

"We're going to be married, Skye," he told her, kneeling on their coats which he'd spread out on the floor, patting the space beside him.

It was difficult for her; painful and awkward. She was glad for the alcohol — *the devil's handmaiden*, according to her mother. She worried the whole time about consequences.

"It's okay," he whispered, when she said *no*. "I love you," he said, kissing her ears and neck when she said *yes*.

Skye lowered her skirt from above her waist where he'd hiked it. She placed her head on his chest and could hear his heart pounding.

"I'm so happy," he said. "I'm the luckiest guy in the world."

"Me too," she lied. "Me too," she whispered, trusting that someday she'd believe what she said.

She fell asleep and after a few minutes was awakened by Rory using the toilet. She wanted to plug her ears. She was embarrassed at the sound of his urinating; she gathered that there would be a series of new noises that would come with marriage, but she wasn't ready for them yet.

"Skye," he said, "come in here."

"Rory," she giggled, "We are pushing our luck. There is security in this building, you know."

In spite of her nerves, Skye picked her coat off the floor, shook out the wrinkles and put it on. She left her stockings and panties on the floor, and tiptoed through the dark to the cubicle where Rory stood zipping up his pants.

"What in the devil are you up to?" she asked, giggly at the thought of being a willing participant in mischief.

"I'll do my initials and you do yours," he said, pointing to the wall behind the toilet. "We should try to hide them, though."

Rory removed the lid off the toilet tank. "Do you have anything sharp we can use?"

Skye didn't have to think too long; she unpinned her grouse-feet brooch from the collar of her coat and handed it to Rory. "We can use the pin," she said.

Rory etched an *R* followed by another into the wood. He handed her the brooch and said *forever*.

She placed her initials above his and then together they put the lid back on the tank, hiding their secret. *Forever*, she said, placing the brooch in her coat pocket.

"Let's get out of here," she said. "My mother will have my head …."

# EDINBURGH, 2011

Duncan sits next to Siobhan in the dark of the Anatomy Lecture Room looking at images of a female and two male dancers moving slowly on three giant screens in front of them, trying to imagine what Skye would have been like back then. He is trying to compose himself before going back into the Dissection Room bar to find Paul again. Every room and corridor is being used for the Festival; the old building is alive with art. At first he thinks they're just photographs of dancers but then he sees an arm move, a foot, and gradually a smile on one of the faces. The images seem alive, he can almost hear their breathing, smell their flesh. The result is so sensual that it's almost religious. Mesmerized, Duncan thinks about Skye and how she was over-the-moon thrilled when he told her that he'd been accepted to the Edinburgh Festival; they'd talked for months about things he should do in the city. *Buy a guide! Go to Arthur's Seat*, she said. *Of course the city will have changed a great deal since my day. And at Summerhall*, she'd whispered, *explore every crook and cranny. If only those walls could talk.*

When he teaches, he's attentive to his students. And when he is doing a portrait, he's attentive to his imagination, but there's something about the images on the wall in front of him that reminds him that every day he is surrounded by talking, walking human beings — each with a heart and a brain. The photo images continue to roll across the screen; darkness and an unnerving smell absorbed into the walls and old wooden benches challenge his senses.

"That smell is nauseating," says Siobhan. "What is it?"

"I was just thinking the same thing," he says. "Probably formaldehyde or chloroform, something they would have used on the animals back then."

"These images are gorgeous," she says, "but it's kind of spooky in this place. How are you doing?"

He wants to get back to the Dissecting Room bar where Paul is waiting, but he still feels strange, not able to shake off the feeling that Skye is somehow present.

"Something's up with Skye."

Determined to go with Duncan for his first art show, Siobhan is staying at a students' residence near Summerhall. He called her to let her know about the date with Paul. He was excited. She was more excited.

"I think you should get her off your brain," she says. "You didn't fly to the other side of the ocean to meet someone and then spend your time thinking about Skye."

"It's a first date, Siobhan. Don't marry us off yet."

"Who is he?" she asks. "Where did you meet?"

"He's a really nice guy who has a show going on here too. I met him at a place called the Blue Moon."

No sooner do the words come out of his mouth than Duncan is overcome with the feeling that something is brushing up against him. He can't see in the dark and he wants to run; instead, he closes his eyes, tries to focus. When he opens them again, there are waves of orange, blue and green above his head and along the walls, like the northern lights.

"I can hear her voice," he tells Siobhan.

"You're scaring me," she says. "You're either stoned or totally psychotic."

"Neither," he says. "Something is wrong with Skye."

"You spend too much time with her," Siobhan says. "This trip couldn't have happened soon enough."

# KINCARDINE, 2011

Skye can smell the smoke but can't get up. The pain in her chest is worse and she can't move her arms or legs. She tries to ease her head off the table; she's able to move an inch, then another, and another inch, until her head and shoulders flop off the edge. But rather than slide back into the chair as she'd hoped, she becomes unbalanced and falls over onto the floor. *Oh my.* She is surprised to hear the words leave her mouth. *Duncan.*

# EDINBURGH, 2011

The giant images flash over and over again, the dancers move slowly. A woman lifts one leg above her head; on either side of her, the two shirtless men turn, bend and straighten, look out to Duncan watching back in the dark.

"Do you remember the time we played the Ouija board in the basement of your house?" Siobhan whispers.

"Don't make things spookier than they are already, Siobhan," he says. "And why are you whispering? There's no one else in here."

"Don't you remember? Skye was out delivering a cow or gelding some stallion and we made our own board out of plywood and magic markers."

"And we both kept laughing and giggling and were afraid of pissing the spirits off, but couldn't stop."

"And we were trying to balance the board on our knees and it kept falling."

"Do you remember the question we asked it?"

"We asked if the spirit was from the sun or the moon."

"But after that?"

"Not really," says Siobhan. "I just remember cracking up."

"We asked if I was going to find true love!"

"Oh GOD!!" Siobhan says. "And the spirit said no."

"And then it said yes!"

"And then we heard Skye come in and we had to blow out the candles and hide the Ouija board and she came into your room and thought we were making out because the lights were off."

"She knows better now," says Duncan. "She knows a lot, and I think she's trying to tell me something now."

"Duncan," Siobhan says. "You're being really weird. We should probably get you to a doctor."

"I don't need a doctor," Duncan says. "Something's up with Skye."

"She's on the other side of the ocean, Duncan. You're losing it."

Duncan stands and pushes past Siobhan in the dark. "Are you coming or not?"

•

As they walk through the crowds of people in the Dissection Room bar, Duncan spots Paul standing by himself with two drinks in his hand.

"No more alcohol for you," Siobhan says, nodding at the drinks in Paul's hands. "You better take it easy for the rest of the night."

"Siobhan, this is Paul. Paul, this is Siobhan," he says.

"Nice to meet you," says Paul. "I almost gave up on you," he says, handing Duncan a beer. "Did you get lost in this crazy old building?"

"Not lost," Duncan says. "I'll tell you later."

"Sorry," says Paul, looking at Siobhan. "I would have bought you a drink had I known."

"I'll have his," Siobhan says, taking Duncan's beer. "He's had enough."

"So," says Paul, looking at Siobhan, "Duncan says you are best buds?"

Siobhan has never been quiet or shy in her life, but she's flustered.

"Yeah," she says.

The music is loud and the three of them stand close, none of them able to make conversation.

"I'll go get some water for Duncan," Paul says, and starts walking back to the bar.

"He's bloody gorgeous," Siobhan says, once Paul is out of earshot.

•

The Dissection Room looks different in the light — the walls seem brighter and the posters of animals are more playful than sinister. The room has a contemporary feel to it that is reassuring — even the glass cases with their well-lit displays of teeth and bones seem to be harmless relics more grounded in dusty old science than the spirit world. They were asked to arrive just before the doors opened to the public at 7:00, but Duncan, chronically early for everything, arrives at 6:15.

"I guess I'm the first," he says to Rupert, the show's curator whom he recognizes from his picture on Summerhall's website. "This is my friend from Kincardine, Siobhan."

"Welcome to Scotland," says Rupert, looking at Duncan, then over to Siobhan. "Susan is here as well. She's just stepped out for a cigarette."

Rupert is about Duncan's age, tall and thin with bare feet in sandals, loose-fitting clothing, and dark, braided hair pulled back in a ponytail. No sooner does he say her name than Susan McDougall appears next to them. She's an older woman with silver hair and blue eyes — the intense blue that belong to every clichéd version of the possessed and passionate artist that has ever existed. Duncan extends his hand to shakes hers and she holds it for several seconds.

"Your drawings are beautiful and powerful, Duncan. It's a pleasure to meet you. And you as well," she adds, shaking Siobhan's hand.

Duncan immediately relaxes. He had been worried about meeting other artists — especially seasoned artists like Susan McDougall and Mark Montreal. They walk with Susan and Rupert into the Dissection Room with a big sign above the entry: *Northern Lights at Summerhall.*

"There must be a lot of disembodied animals roaming this room," says Duncan. "Some say you will never see a bird flying over Summerhall because they can see and smell the spirits of all the dead animals from here. Is that true?" he asks.

"The rumours are true," Rupert answers. "This is a strange and wonderful old building."

At about head height, a narrow shelf has been placed around the main part of the room and on it are Susan McDougall's head sculptures like a tribe of bodiless ghosts. And hanging above these haunted and enigmatic casts are Mark Montreal's paintings. Duncan focuses on the painting closest to him. It's a collage of Icarus fallen from the sun and Poseidon standing over him with his trident. As he gets closer, Duncan can see the waxy wings and naked subject face down; the trident's forks consist of three penises pointed at the fallen boy.

"I love it," says Siobhan.

"I love it too," Duncan lies.

For Duncan's drawings, the curator has set up four large tables in the centre of the room; the sofas and chairs have been removed and the bar looks and feels like a contemporary art gallery. Duncan had sent Rupert twenty drawings for the show. The drawings were mounted and matted in neutral colours but, at Duncan's request, they were not framed. Each drawing is the same size: sixty by seventy-five centimetres. The dimensions, price and title of each drawing are placed along the side as well as his name.

Siobhan reads the first one out loud: "Duncan Johnson, Toronto, Canada, *Ox and Fox*: sixty by seventy-five centimetres. They always put Toronto," she says.

"Well, people really don't know where Kincardine is," says Duncan.

"People from Scotland will know," she insists. "Ninety percent of Kincardine is populated by old Scots."

"Sorry," says Rupert. "I'd never heard of Kincardine in Canada."

When Mark Montreal walks into the room a few minutes later, it's as if a cloud has been pushed in by a strong wind — Duncan feels chilled, gets goosebumps on his skin as he looks at the overweight artist with the pasty white skin, big nose and piss-yellow aura.

"Anthropomorphizing animals brings me back to my youth," he says, stroking his goatee while staring at *Ox and Fox*. "The kind of thing my high school art teacher would have made us do."

"I am a high school art teacher," says Duncan, extending his hand, regretting his attempt to downplay Montreal's comment.

"There we go," Montreal says, ignoring Duncan's hand. "I guess you don't do colour?" Montreal doesn't wait for an answer. "A little repressed, I'd say. Overly allegorical."

"Is your name really Montreal?" Siobhan asks, stepping between Duncan and Mark Montreal.

"Are you kidding?" Montreal answers, walking away.

"What's your problem!?" she says to his back.

Duncan eases away from the others and stands in front of one of Mark Montreal's paintings. Without a doubt, it is one of the best paintings he has ever seen — the reference to classic art without being nostalgic. Line, light and colour in perfect balance while managing to look off kilter and daring. Extraordinary technique, each image flying off the page. *Fuck you, Mark Montreal,* he whispers.

"You?" Siobhan says. "Duncan Johnson swore out loud."

"He's not very nice," Duncan says as Susan McDougall joins them.

"Welcome to the cold, cruel world of art shows," she teases.

•

When he gets back to the hotel, Duncan drops his wet umbrella on the floor next to the bed and grabs his sketch pad out of his backpack. He is worried about Skye, but pushes her out of his thoughts. He sits at the desk and, one by one, he carefully places tubes of oil colours next to his sketch pad. He isn't going to wait for a proper canvas or for the set of brushes he will need for the details of his painting: *Strike while the iron is hot,* he hears Skye's voice. Duncan always wanted to paint something like Bosch's *Garden of Earthly Delights*, but didn't feel that Kincardine was ready for the shock of an orgy or explicit eroticized damnation. After the encounter with Mark Montreal, Duncan is ready to let his brushes fly. He draws Montreal as a warthog, his famous goatee and ponytail in every image. He draws him more obese than he is in real life, emphasizing the rolls of fat and the redness of his bulbous nose. Without editing, stopping or thinking, he works all night, squeezing red onto the painting and orange and pink and green and yellow. He draws fantastical animals and enormous fruit; his hellscape has Mark Montreal eternally indulgent and burning. And when the sun comes through the window in the morning, Duncan is pleased: *Hieronymus Hog*, he writes across the top of the painting, then drops the brush in the trash can by the desk. All his years of instructing his students to be expressive and take creative risks. All those mornings with Skye at the kitchen table telling her to let loose, think outside of the lines — Duncan realizes he has been playing it safe. *Thank you, Mark Montreal.* He's ready to break out of his shell.

•

The night of the party at the Dissection Room, they escorted Siobhan back to her room at the Chalmers residence, and then walked in the rain to Charlotte Square. Paul mostly talked about art; Duncan talked about his life growing up in a small town with Skye.

"She's eccentric and funny," he said. "Kincardine doesn't know what to make of her."

"You really like your grandmother," Paul said, a hint of sarcasm in his voice.

"Yes," said Duncan, aware that he had been talking about Skye, non-stop. "She taught me everything."

"Everything?"

"Pretty much," said Duncan, and they walked in silence for a while.

"Do you want to come back to my place for a puff?" asked Paul. "I live close by and we can get out of these wet clothes."

Duncan's heart began to race. Paul wasn't the subtle type, and the thought of taking his clothes off with him was exciting and terrifying.

"No, thanks," he said. "Siobhan, on the other hand, would have smoked her brains out with you, had she known."

"It's you I'm hot after, Duncan," Paul said. And right there, against a tree in Charlotte Square, they had their first kiss with rain streaming down and someone honking their horn as they splashed by.

•

Aside from the fact that he lived on the other side of the ocean, everything about Paul seemed perfect. The bed sheets had fallen to the floor and they were naked. Paul had his head on Duncan's chest, and Duncan had his hand on Paul's neck.

"Don't move," Duncan said, "There's a spider on your neck."

"Get it!" said Paul. "I'm allergic."

Duncan tickled the back of Paul's neck, walked his fingers down to the top of his shoulders. "There once was a spider …" he began.

•

"It's bad luck to harm a spider," Skye said.

They were in the backyard. He was twelve, and earning his allowance by cutting the grass that hadn't been cut for weeks. It was a sunny September morning, and Duncan pulled back a rock so that he could trim the grass at its edges.

"Don't do that," she insisted, when she saw him stamping on a spider.

"There's a gazillion of them here," he said, using the tip of the shears to point. "They'll get in the house."

"Let me tell you about a spider," she said, "come." Skye motioned him to sit beside her on the blanket where she'd been reading the newspaper.

"I'm too old for fairy tales now," he said.

"But this isn't a fairy tale," she said, as he sat down beside her. "This really happened."

"I'm hot," he said, wiping sweat from his face with the end of the blanket.

"Lie back then. Cool down."

As Duncan listened, Skye became progressively more animated. She stood, hunched her back, waved her arms...the spider in her story was enormous and had a skull-and-crossbone image on its abdomen. It looked like a poisonous variety because of its colour and yellow markings, but at the end of her story it saved the day.

"How's that possible?" he asked her, when she got to the part of her story where the spider spun a web around the nose and mouth of the evil Nazi spy as he slept, causing him to suffocate.

"It happened," she said. "It happened in Scotland when I was a girl. Everyone in Edinburgh knows this story. No one went to the spy's funeral. As a matter of fact, there wasn't a funeral, they burned his body in a pit, then threw it into the sea, causing four days of rain."

"That's ridiculous, Grandma Skye," he'd told her. "I'm not a kid anymore. I don't believe everything you say."

But he had bad dreams that night, and every night that week. He was ashamed to tell her that he'd become terrified of spiders. His nights were full of them, and he sought them out during the day to kill them. And when Skye finally figured out why he looked so tired, she promised to tell him when she was having fun, or pulling his leg.

•

"...that spider," he said, continuing to walk his fingers down Paul's back, "...killed off Nazis like they were flies. That's why it's bad to hurt them."

"Another one of your grandmother's stories?" Paul sighed, and stared up at the ceiling.

Duncan had told him about crow's feet pie earlier.

"No. I didn't hear this from Skye," he said, instantly regretting the lie.

"Sounds like one of those war stories the old people around here tell."

Growing up, there were days when Duncan was proud to be raised by Skye; everyone in town knew she was the best veterinarian in the county, everyone knew how strong and smart she was. When Thistle got sick, Skye made him fresh chicken every day and taught Duncan how to give him his insulin. When the kids at school teased him because his drawings were *weird* or because he was shy, Skye always had a story that made him feel better.

"I lied," he told Paul. "Skye did tell me that spider story."

Paul rolled on top of him and started kissing him hard. "I guess I'm a little jealous," he said, tickling his ribs.

It never occurred to Duncan that someone could envy his life with Skye. Until Paul, he hadn't given much thought to life without her, either.

•

Light was coming into the room, and it took Duncan a few seconds to realize where he was. Finally, the rain had stopped — *Scottish mist*, the locals call it. Paul wasn't in the bed, but Duncan could hear him in the kitchen.

Duncan dozed off and when he opened his eyes again, Paul was standing next to the bed with two cups of coffee.

"Listen, Paul," he said, rubbing his eyes. "The last thing I thought was going to happen in Scotland was a fling…I have to get back to Canada."

"A fling?" said Paul. "It doesn't have to be *a fling*."

"We live three thousand miles apart," he said. "And Skye… well, she's old and I promised I'd be back."

"Duncan," Paul said, taking his hand. "Let's face it, your grandmother isn't going to be here much longer. This is a once-in-a-lifetime chance. I know we've just met, but you care for me. I can tell."

Paul pulled him closer and Duncan began to soften. "Look at me," he said. "Tell me you don't care."

Duncan didn't answer; he looked at Paul's face. He was pretty amazing, and hot, and talented… He'd never met anyone like him in Kincardine.

"We were meant to be," said Paul. "I know I sound like a melodramatic fool, but did you know that North America and Great Britain were once one joined at the hip, as they say?"

Duncan knew his geography, but hadn't given the planet's plate shifting too much thought.

"Yes," said Paul. "Edinburgh is a dead volcano. Arthur's Seat, or …as you like to call it, Harry's…was the tip."

Duncan thought of Skye, old and alone. "I don't think so, Paul," he said. "I have to get home. I have a job, students who count on me."

"The Black Cuillin, on the Isle of Skye, was the biggest volcano this planet has ever seen," Paul said, kissing Duncan on the lips. "I'm crazy for you."

Way too fast, Duncan thought. That was way too fast. Who says *I'm crazy for you* after two dates?

"Paul…" he said, feeling confused.

•

"Did you hear?" said Siobhan when Duncan finally reached her on her cellphone. "Jack Layton's dead. I just got an e-mail…"

"Siobhan?" he said. "That's really sad news, but there's something else. Can we meet for coffee?"

"Sure," she said, "what's wrong?"

"I don't know if something is *wrong*," he said, "but Paul wants me to move here."

"OMG!" said Siobhan. "You've slept with him."

"How about meeting me at the Blue Moon in an hour?"

"An hour and a half," she said. "I have…urghmm…company right now."

•

Duncan thought about Paul as he walked over North Bridge. He stopped to examine a mass of purple moving slowly across the horizon like clouds in a Turner painting, billowing and robust, the way he thought all clouds would look in Scotland. *Scottish mist*, he sighed, as the rain streamed down and his knees buckled under him.

# PART V

# KINCARDINE, 2011

The water begins to boil for her porridge. Skye can hear the soft rumble and splashing on the stove. She starts to stand, but feels dizzy. *Squirrely Shirley,* they called her. *Shirley Kellins* from Tiverton.

## KINCARDINE, 1965

"All the other mothers dress nice. All the other mothers go to the hairdresser. All the other mothers ..."

"Enough about all the other mothers," Skye told Moira. "I'm not all the other mothers, so you might as well get used to it. Now why are you so upset?"

"What do you care?" Moira said. "I'm not a cat or a dog or a horse."

Moira had turned fifteen and the world was changing fast — everything in her day revolved around appearance and boys.

# KINCARDINE, 1966

When Skye turned on the light and found Moira's bed empty, she wasn't completely surprised. She knew well enough that Moira was capable of disobedience; however, she was genuinely taken aback when she noticed the dresser drawers flung open and the clothes closet empty — even the gold silk cover that she'd kept on the foot of her bed since she was a baby was gone. Skye ran back down the hallway to the bedroom.

"Wake up, Rory," she said. "Moira's snuck out."

Skye had assumed that Moira would go to her boyfriend's, but she had no idea what Magnus's last name was.

"I don't think she ever told us," Rory said.

"Figures," said Skye.

She and Rory drove up and down the dark streets looking for her until Rory finally insisted they go home.

"We both have to work tomorrow," he said. "She'll be all right."

"That girl doesn't think of anyone but herself," Skye said. "She's grounded for a month."

"I think we had better wait until she gets home safely before you start your next plan of discipline," Rory said.

"You're no help. Why am I always the bad one?"

They learned about Moira's plan to live with Magnus through a letter slipped into the front-door mail slot three days later.

"She must have delivered it at some point in the night," Rory said, handing Skye the white envelope. "She's moved in with him. Most of what she writes is for you."

"I'm not reading it," Skye told him. "Throw it out."

"I think you should," he said. "This is our one and only child."

"She's not mine anymore," Skye said, aware of how excessive her words were for the situation and how much she sounded like her own mother.

"Your feelings are hurt right now, Skye," Rory said. "But you'll regret it if you don't read what she has to say. Our daughter needs a mother right now."

"It's late, Rory. Please. I don't have time for her rebellious antics."

"I'll put it here," he said, gently placing the envelope on the kitchen table. "Read it when you calm down."

•

Magnus and Moira had dated on-and-off for two years, but Moira couldn't make up her mind. They were walking down Saugeen Street to Lovers' Lane.

"You're acting particularly romantic tonight, Magnus Johnson," she said, kicking sand on the path with her bare feet. "What did you do all day?"

"It's a perfect night, Moira," he said, looking out at an orange sunset on the lake. "And look at these," he added. "Wild roses."

He snapped off a flower and handed it to her.

Moira had a temper, but she wasn't one to stay mad for long. They'd had a fight over breakfast. They were late for the rent and Moira had thrown up twice that morning.

"No more partying for me," she'd moaned, with her head hanging over the toilet. "You make your own breakfast today," she yelled from the bathroom.

Over coffee, she told him that her parents thought he was a loser.

"Did they really say that?"

"Not actually, but Dad keeps asking if you've found a job yet. And Mom keeps asking if I'm *taking precautions*."

He'd spent the day trying to figure out what to do — they could move to the city where there were more jobs. They could move to Alberta; there was an oil boom out there. He could apply at the plant? That's it! He could tell them that he'd finish his high school at night, explain that he was a hard worker who could do anything. He'd be the best worker that nuclear plant ever had.

He took his guitar to a pawn shop in Toronto, where he'd also bought the ring.

She took the rose in one hand; he held her other hand and dropped to his knees. "Moira Rayburn," he said, letting go of her hand and fishing for the ring he'd stuffed into his pants pocket, "will you marry me?"

He knew in his gut that she'd probably say no, so he thought he'd let her off the hook.

"It doesn't have to be tomorrow or this year or next year for that matter," he said. "Just as long as it's sometime."

"Oh, Magnus. You don't have a job. I don't have a job. I don't even think it's legal."

By then they'd come out of Lovers' Lane, by the town garden. Moira sat down on a rock and folded her hands in her lap.

"Sit here," she said, patting a large, round boulder beside her. "Brace yourself."

•

Magnus was genuinely shocked to hear that Moira was pregnant; she'd told him she was on the pill, and he knew that she didn't want kids. He sat on the boulder and watched the last streak of orange sky disappear on the horizon. The temperature had dropped dramatically, and waves formed across the lake. Moira hadn't answered his question, and she wouldn't look at him when he'd asked her again.

"I'm sorry," said Moira. "I missed a few days, I guess."

"I asked before I knew this," he said. "People will think we got married because of the baby, but we'll both always know that I asked before I knew."

"It's getting cold," she said. "Now that the sun's gone down."

"Let's go," he said. "You don't have to answer me now."

"I'm sixteen years old, Magnus. What do you think the answer is?"

•

Years later, after Moira had died, Skye pulled out *Life Lessons for Duncan* and something in the back of the drawer caught her eye that almost caused her to faint — it was Moira's letter with her teenage girl's handwriting, *for Mom and Dad,* scribbled on the front.

Skye placed both hands on the kitchen table and inhaled deeply to steady her nerves. Then she carefully tore open the envelope.

*Dear Mom,* the letter begins. *I know this is going to hurt you a lot, but I am moving in with Magnus. And I'm glad. No more "go do your homework." No "straighten up your room." No "make something of yourself." No more, "You're ruining your life, Moira."*

*I'm going to Montreal, there's a women's clinic there. I'm too young for a kid and Magnus would be a useless father. I'm smarter than you think, Mom,* she wrote. *I'll get it together soon enough. And when I have a baby for keeps, I'll tell him: Love yourself; love someone else — no rules but that.*

*Dear Dad,* she wrote. *Good luck.*

# KINCARDINE, 1981

Moira was inconsolable when her father died. She cried and acted as if his passing was Skye's fault.

"You could have told me," she shouted. "How long did you wait before you called?"

Skye couldn't do it. She couldn't leave his side, accept the hard, cold fact that they'd come with a stretcher, covered him up and taken him away.

"I called you the minute I had the strength to," she said.

"Well, now that I'm here, we'd better call Davey-Linklater," Moira said, her voice a little softer.

"Come here, Moira," Skye said, patting the bed where she was sitting next to Rory. "I've called them already."

"I'd rather not see him like that," Moira said. "That's not how I want to remember him," she added, nodding at one of Rory's grey-blue feet sticking out from under the covers.

"You're right," said Skye, pulling the sheet down to cover him completely. "His soul is somewhere else now. But his spirit is still with us. I feel it, Moira. He's here. He wouldn't want us to fight."

Skye shifted over so Moira could sit next to her. She put her arms around her daughter, and when Moira rested her head on her shoulders, Skye pushed back her hair and kissed the top of her head. They wept until the hearse pulled up in front of the house and the doorbell rang.

"Where's Magnus?" Skye asked, innocently.

Moira stood abruptly and turned to her mother. "He's at work, Mother," she said. "You know he got a job a few weeks ago."

•

Rory's funeral was held at Davey-Linklater Funeral Home. It was early summer and there was a calm, cloudless sky. It was a bittersweet moment for everyone, as Moira had announced her pregnancy a few days before. They were glad that Rory had lived to hear the news, but bent with grief over his passing. Magnus sat next to Moira in the front row, sober and proud. The room was full, not a seat to be found, and Skye told them all the story of how they met.

"The war had just ended," she said, "and he was a handsome devil…"

Skye had no trouble speaking, she had had time to adjust to his passing and she knew the real grief would come when she was alone in the house without him.

"Rory Rayburn was a loyal friend to many in this town," she said. "And a good father by anyone's standards."

# KINCARDINE, 1984

The night of the accident Moira had agreed to be the designated driver. Magnus had been watching the booze, but it was his birthday and Skye had agreed to babysit. They'd heard that there might be a blizzard, but as they headed toward Toronto, there wasn't a snowflake in the sky. Moira was happy to be away from Skye's nagging: *You're a mother now, and you need to start behaving as such.* And Magnus was just happy to be with her; since the baby was born, Moira hadn't shown him too much affection.

They ate dinner at the Keg, even though it was more than he could afford. They took their time and shared a piece of chocolate cake and watched the snow falling outside the window that faced Jarvis Street. After the birthday cake, they shared a second bottle of wine and took a taxi over to the Brunswick House for a few birthday beers.

After one beer Moira said she would start drinking coffee. But when the waiter came, she ordered another pint. Magnus ordered coffee. "You promised," he said, "and the snow's getting worse."

"I know those Bruce County side roads like the back of my hand," she'd said. "Besides, the O.P.P. never leave 21."

After last call, they flagged a taxi back to the Keg to pick up the car. Moira started to brush snow off the windshield, but slipped on the ice.

"Maybe we should find some cheap place in the city?" he said.

"I'm capable of driving, Magnus," she'd said. "Besides, Skye will have a bird."

She was slurring her words, and slipped on the ice again trying to get into the car on the driver's side.

"Give me the keys," he said. "You're piss drunk."

"Jerk," she said, throwing him the keys.

Getting out of the city wasn't too bad. The roads were mostly salted and the highways were pretty good with no sign of police. Magnus thought for sure they'd be all right.

"Get off here," Moira said, when the exit for Side Road 3 came up at Mildmay. "We can hook onto 9 from here."

She seemed even more drunk than when they'd first got into the car, and Magnus panicked when he saw her drinking from a bottle of beer that she must have snuck from the bar.

"Are you crazy?" he yelled. "Do you know what the fine is for open booze in a car?"

He poured what was left of the beer out the window and tucked the empty bottle under his seat. Moira tried to turn up the temperature, but the heater was broken. She wrapped her coat tightly around herself, pulled the collar up to her chin and crouched lower in the seat. Soon after, she fell asleep with her head against the icy window.

The traffic was moving, although pretty slowly. Magnus felt happy to be close to her and forgot about being mad as he drove through the snow. He looked forward to being in bed next to her, and to kissing Duncan on the forehead as they passed by his bedroom on the way to theirs.

At Rockysdale, the wind picked up and the drifting got worse.

"Moira," he whispered. "Wake up. I can hardly see the road."

"What do you expect me to do about it," she mumbled, pulling her coat up over her head and sinking down in the seat. "I was sleeping, ya know."

Magnus turned the radio up and rolled down the window. He needed to keep his wits about him. The windshield wipers weren't keeping up with the snow, and he wanted to pull over to chip the ice off the back window, but he'd heard about too many accidents that happened after other drivers pulled over during a whiteout. Where the road ended and where the field began became a blur by the time they got to Bervie, and he slowed down to practically ten miles an hour. And when he turned the corner at Millarton, between the snow blowing across the field, and the curve of the road, Magnus couldn't possibly have seen the truck that slammed into them, head on.

•

There aren't many people at Davey-Linklater. A few friends that Moira went to school with, and four or five members of Magnus's family sit in chairs and sofas scattered about the reception room.

"Sky with an e on the end," she says. This day, of all days, she finds it hard to muster the energy to explain.

"It sounds like a hippie name," says Magnus's father, who sat down next to her on the sofa with a stinky egg salad sandwich.

*And it's not nice to speak with your mouth full* is what she wants to tell him, but instead she says: "It's not meant to be a 'hippie' name."

"Oh?" he says.

"I am named after the Isle of Skye, in Scotland, where I was born."

"Oh," the man says, taking another bite of his sandwich.

Skye follows the staff member who asks them to move into the chapel. She is relieved that Magnus's father stays put. Once everyone is seated, Cathy walks up to the microphone and sighs, brushing her long black hair back with one hand, holding a piece of paper with the other. Skye doesn't know much about Cathy, but she remembers that she's the one that Moira used to get into trouble with.

"Good morning, everyone," she says, red in the face, choking back tears. "I never thought that I would be here before Moira."

Skye holds her breath and looks out the window. It's a perfect winter day, clear and crisp, without clouds. Tiny ice particles form along the inside edges of the window where she sits with Magnus and his mother and father. Duncan is outside playing in the snow; one of the staff members said he'd keep his eye on him. He'd refused to come inside, and Skye didn't feel like forcing him to sit through the service.

"How's he doing?" Cathy asked when she first arrived. Skye had been standing on the steps at the entrance to the funeral home, breathing in the cool air, thinking back to the day that they buried Rory.

"Night time is difficult for him," Skye told her. "But he is resilient, a happy child."

Then Cathy gave her that look. The same smirk that Moira used to give her — confusion mixed with anger, a frown with an upturned edge.

"I'm glad he's a happy kid," she'd said. "Hope he stays that way."

Skye knew the comment was meant to hurt her. Cathy was the girl in town who got pregnant at fifteen. She was the one who smoked pot and was kicked out of school, the girl that she tried to keep Moira from socializing with.

•

Cathy looks over to the pink satin-lined casket. Her voice changes from grief-stricken to angry in two seconds flat.

"Moira was my best friend," she says. "She was an angel — the good one. I was the bad kid destined for trouble."

"I'll say," her father says, not attempting to lower his voice. He and his wife are sitting on the far end of the row, next to Magnus's father, and the mother who hasn't spoken since she arrived. Magnus is next to Skye, staring at the ground, motionless and horrifically stiff. From time to time, she looks over to see if he's still breathing.

"Moira was the one who could have had it all."

Magnus flinches, as if he has been pinched. Then he settles again into his catatonic stupor.

"She leaves behind a child and a husband. She's in heaven now," Cathy says. "If there's such a place."

Unnecessary, Skye thinks. This cynical edge has no place at a funeral. She prays that Cathy will wrap up soon.

"You should probably check on Duncan," Skye whispers, but Magnus is held by Cathy's words.

"When we were young," she says. "Moira got B's and I got D's, but she still couldn't make some people happy."

This comment is directed at her as well. *You complain about wanting to get out of this town…*Skye used to tell Moira …*B's and C's won't cut it at U of T.*

"Moira joined the swimming team and volunteered at the community centre. I sat and watched her swim. I've never volunteered for a thing in my life."

Where's all this going? Skye wonders.

"And look where it got her. Dead because of something stupid."

Skye slides her arm under Magnus's and pulls him closer. "You don't have to hear this," she whispers.

"Shhhh," he says.

"Something stupid, but at least she was happy for a change."

*Ah,* thinks Skye.

"Moira never got to do anything fun in her life. She finished school because she was obedient. She got married and had a kid, 'cause that's what you do in this place. But at least she had fun before the accident. Right, Mag?" she yells across the room. "She went out with a smile."

Magnus stands to leave. "Goin' to check on Duncan," he whispers to Skye.

She tries to keep her eyes on Cathy, but she is also watching Magnus through the window kneeling down next to Duncan. The Davey-Linklater staff member steps back and Magnus hugs Duncan for a long time. Then Duncan points to the snowman he's been building. Magnus pulls something orange from his pocket and creates a nose for the snowman. He shakes snow off a bush and uses two skinny twigs for arms. Duncan jumps up and down, Magnus hugs him again and leaves. Skye wonders if this will be the last she sees of him, but Duncan seems oblivious to his father's departure. On his back, he waves his arms and legs in the snow, while the young man from Davey-Linklater steps back a few feet, lights a cigarette and looks toward the window. It's hard for Skye to see now because of tears. It's hard to believe this is all possible. She takes her purse from her lap and sets it on the bench where Magnus had been sitting. There's music playing, something that Cathy picked for Moira. *Yes, I'm let loose from the noose ...*

There's quiet laughter when Cathy speaks over the music: "Me and Moira used to dance our butts off to AC/DC," she says as the song continues.

*Forget the hearse 'cause I never die I got nine lives, cat's eyes.*

Then, looking over, Cathy says something that cracks Skye wide open.

"Me and Moira and her mom even threw back a few beers to this song once, when we all figured what the hell, life's got to have some fun in it sometimes."

Skye picks up her purse and holds it close. She bends over and sobs. She cries for a long time and when she lifts her head Duncan is standing next to her. Cathy is holding his hand. The hand that she is holding still has its red mitten; the other hand is bare and Skye can see the red string of wool hanging from his coat sleeve. She'd put those mittens on a string and slid them through his coat sleeves after he'd lost his second pair in as many weeks.

"Look what we made for the snowman's nose," he says, holding out the gold cigarette lighter.

"*Used* for the snowman's nose, not *made*," she says. "The lighter was already made. And what happened to your other mitten?"

Cathy lets go of Duncan's hand, kisses him on the cheek and walks away, but not without a look that could have brought down a mountain — her nonverbal retaliation against what Moira once called *Mother's Adolf Hitler regime.*

Skye pulls her wedding ring off her right-hand finger and squeezes it onto the left, reminds herself to find the lyrics to that song. She'd never *throw back a few beers* with that girl if her life depended on it, she thinks, as she takes Duncan's small, cold hand in hers.

•

As they walked down the front steps of Davey-Linklater, she saw Duncan's lost mitten, a crimson smudge in the snow. She picked it up and squeezed it, half frozen, onto Duncan's hand. Together they walked directly to the house on Princes Street. She put him down for a nap in her bed and called Rosemary Newman, next door, to come over and watch him. She walked the four blocks to the Royal Apartments where Moira and Magnus lived. The apartments were originally built to house the women who worked at the knitting mill; they weren't all that fancy, but they were convenient, cheap, and available when they needed a place most. She let herself in with the key under the rock at the side door. Skye knew Moira was no great homemaker and that Magnus had never washed a dish or lifted a mop in his life, but she wasn't prepared for Duncan's bedroom. The smell just about knocked her over. Moira had been training him to use the potty, and it looked like he'd used it a few times. There was a bag of bread on the floor, chewed opened by mice, a bag of spilled potato chips and a few cans of cola. The bed wasn't made and the dresser was empty; all of Duncan's clothes and toys were scattered around the floor. At first, she didn't go into their bedroom; she wanted to remember Moira better than that. Instead, she went into the kitchen to see if there was food to be thrown out of the refrigerator or dishes to be done. She tidied a little and put the garbage by the door and went back into Duncan's bedroom. She picked up his stuffed purple dragon and a few of his trucks and cars, put a pile of his clothes in a green garbage bag and closed the bedroom door behind her. She'd come back for the bed and a few more clothes, and to check with landlord about rental arrears.

Skye cleaned out the fridge and washed the dishes. She dried her hands on her skirt because the towel was dirty and walked down the hall to their bedroom. She cracked the bedroom door open slowly, but had to push because there was something blocking the way. Then she heard a moan, a woman's voice: *Is that you Magnus?* The woman was naked except for her bra and shorts, and from what Skye could see from the crack in the doorway, she'd been there for a day or two. There were beer bottles and leftover Chinese food scattered across the floor, as well as blankets, pillows, clothing; even the curtains were pulled down from the window.

Skye started to ease the door closed, she didn't say a word. *Mrs. Rayburn?* The woman spoke again. *Skye Rayburn?* the voice asked, *Is that you?*

She didn't answer. Skye marched through the apartment with the bags of clothing hitting her legs. She'd never said it out loud, nor would she ever, but she knew without a doubt that she'd kill him with her bare hands if she ever saw Magnus with Shirley Kellins again — Moira wasn't even cold in the ground.

●

Magnus felt around for the last few coins in his pocket. He'd done his best. He'd tried to find work but couldn't. He tried to be a father to Duncan, but just didn't get it right. He counted the coins and bills and reasoned things out as he walked down the street. He walked toward the highway and hoped for the best — someone who would give him a lift out of town without asking too many questions. He stood on the corner where 9 meets 21, stuck out his thumb and within two minutes he had a lift halfway to Toronto. It was that easy to leave. Skye would take care of Duncan and raise him well, better than he could. She would deal with the Royal Apartments and the mess he'd left there with Shirley. He didn't have a plan for the city, but he knew he'd never see Kincardine again. Maybe he'd find a job. Maybe he'd have to sit out the winter on unemployment. The guy who gave him a ride was visiting friends from high school; he'd never been to Kincardine and liked it. *Where are you from and who do you know in Toronto?* Magnus ignored the questions. *No suitcase or backpack?* he'd said as an observation, not a question, but Magnus took offence. *You sure ask a lot of questions,* he'd said.

*I think I've changed my mind about a passenger,* the driver said when they pulled in for gas at Arthur and Magnus didn't pay for half of the gas as he'd promised. *You shouldn't have a problem getting to Toronto from here.*

But he did have a problem. Magnus had to walk from Arthur to Orangeville. It took him all night and part of the next morning. At

Orangeville he took a bus to Toronto and was grateful to have just the right amount of change for the fare.

*The Seaton House men's shelter is just a few blocks from here*, the security guard who kicked him out of the bus station explained a few hours later.

•

For a long time Duncan cried at bedtime. He asked for his mother and he asked for his father. He wanted his *blankie* and he wanted his old room and his old potty again.

"I'll get that tattered old blanket tomorrow," Skye said, surprised that Moira had managed to keep the gold silk cover her mother had sent over from Scotland. "This is the same thing, Duncan," Skye said, pointing to a newly purchased blue plastic seat. "Now go for Grandma like a good boy."

But he wouldn't tinkle or poop; he just sat there looking up at her, red-faced and crying.

"Okay," she said lifting him, pulling up his pants as he sobbed. "But you have to remember to tell Grandma Skye before you soil yourself next time."

He nodded his head as she wiped his nose, but he would never tell her before going in his shorts. She could usually smell it, and sometimes she could tell by the expression on his face.

"Did you poop?" she would ask and he'd always shake his head *no*.

"Go get me a clean diaper," she'd say as he ran bare-bottomed across the room. "You have to try," she'd yell after him. "You have to let Grandma know."

I don't want this, she'd say to herself. I'm too busy and too old for parenting. Curse that man, she'd say to the photo of Magnus and Moira on the table next to Duncan's bed. *Curse you*, she'd say. Then she looked down at Duncan with the diaper in his hand, smiling and perfect, tugging on her pant leg, and she was grateful.

Then one day, out of the blue, Skye walked into the bathroom next to her bedroom and Duncan was on the toilet. He'd skipped a whole step — he went from refusing to potty train to using the toilet in her washroom.

"Do you need help?" she asked, feeling a little ecstatic.

"No," he said, looking down at his dangling feet.

"After, I'll show you how to build Dunvegan Castle with your Lego," she said, gently closing the bathroom door behind her.

# KINCARDINE, 1985

About a year after Magnus disappeared, Duncan woke up crying. When Skye turned the bedroom light on, she saw him on the bed with the covers kicked back.

"What's the matter, sweet boy?" she asked. "Tell Grandma."

Duncan's face was red and tears streamed down his cheeks. He was still learning to speak in full sentences and at the best of times he couldn't find the right words.

"Do you have a tummy ache?" she asked.

Duncan shook his head, *no*, and turned to face the wall.

"Do you think you ate too many Green Alien eyes?" she asked, gently rubbing his back.

Duncan shook his head, no, again.

One of his favourite treats was green olives, and he had learned the word *alien* from an older child in daycare. *Gween Awian eyes*, he'd insisted, holding one up to his own eye for close examination.

"Don't eat too many," she'd told him. "Green Alien eyes will upset your tummy." But rather than slow down, Duncan reached into the jar, pulling out a tiny fistful of slippery green olives with squashed red pimento centres. Clearly she had lots to learn about raising boys — words that would have made Moira stop eating immediately only fuelled Duncan's delight. Laughing and stuffing his little mouth, he ran around the living room pretending to be an alien. He roared and growled, then spat the half-eaten olives back into the jar from which they'd come.

"Don't do that, Duncan. Bad," she said as if she were scolding a misbehaving pet. "Bad, bad boy!"

She thought back to a heavily pregnant cow she had treated a week earlier. The gas in the rumen had built up and because of her delayed pregnancy she was wide as a house. She was a show cow and the farmer was very upset. Skye could see an apple inside the throat, but could not dislodge it. She put on gloves, and placed a small block of wood between the cow's jaw, cursing as she reached inside. It wasn't easy to grab a wet, slimy, apple from inside a pregnant cow, but she did. And when it was all over, the cow rested her head on her shoulder.

"Open wide," she told Duncan, pulling him onto his back. She'd brought her small flashlight. "Let me look inside."

Duncan wouldn't cooperate. He seemed to be having trouble breathing and he kicked out at her.

"Now behave," she said. "Grandma Skye wants to help."

Duncan's face was red and he was gasping for air.

"Veterinarians know about tummies," she said. "Now let me see what you've put inside."

Duncan was clutching his throat. With her fingers she pried the red-faced child's mouth open. Her intention with the flashlight was more to distract him than anything else, but she thanked the heavens that she'd brought it. Something was caught in his throat. It could be a piece of paper? Perhaps a page from one of his colouring books?

"Don't you move from this bed," she said to Duncan, running down the hall. "What in God's name did you swallow?" she yelled back to the choking child.

In the few seconds that it took for her to locate the pincers in the bottom of her bag and return to his room, Duncan had become semi-conscious and was not moving. His face was blue-grey and his breathing was suspended. She knew that his air passage had become completely blocked. She flipped him onto her knee and pounded as hard as she could with the palm of her hand. Nothing happened and he became limp. She pounded again, and then again, until a small grey object went flying across the floor. Duncan started crying immediately. She held him and rocked him. "It's all right," she told him. "It's all right," she repeated, over and over.

When Duncan finally fell asleep in her arms, she set him down on the bed and covered him with the quilt she'd given Moira when he was born. She walked over and picked a crumpled wad of paper off the floor.

"What the?" she whispered to herself. "What the hell..."

It took a few minutes for her to unfold, but soon enough it became clear that the crumpled object was the picture of Moira and Magnus taken on their wedding day. The one she'd set by Duncan's bedside table.

"They're here on this table," she'd tell Duncan. "Your mama and papa are beside you each night."

What would possess a child to eat a picture? A snake swallows a mouse because it's hungry. A cow eats an apple because it tastes good.

"Why did you do that?" she asked Duncan the next morning as they sat at the kitchen table.

"My thwoat hurts," he said.

"Sip your chocolate milk then," she said. "What did I tell you about putting things in your mouth?"

"I wanted to wemember," he said, shaking, spilling milk onto the table and floor.

"Remember?" Skye said. "Pronounce your R's. You remember your parents by looking at the picture, not by sticking it in your mouth!"

Her voice was overly stern again, but it was too late by the time she realized.

"I'm sorry," she said to the sobbing boy. "I'm sorry," she said, kneeling to wipe milk from the kitchen floor.

# KINCARDINE, 1990

They asked Skye to meet with the social workers first.

"Workers, plural?" she asked over the phone.

"Yes," said the sheriff. "One for the parents, and one for the five children."

"And where is this puppy mill?" asked Skye.

"Off Concession 5 and 23," he told her. "We'll meet you on the corner at nine tomorrow morning."

"Are the animals in the house?" she asked.

"The animals are in a barn behind the house."

"How many?"

"Over a hundred dogs, according to a neighbour, stacked in cages three and four high."

"I'll need help tagging and transporting the animals out of there. And why social workers?" Skye asked, almost afraid to.

"Hoarders. An older couple with problems. The dogs have it bad; the adopted kids have it worse."

"Oh lord," said Skye. "Why do I have to meet with the social workers?"

"The children need to know that the animals are going into good hands. Social Services' logic, not mine."

"Well, tomorrow at nine it is then," she said, and hung up the phone.

•

Skye waited for the officer at the side of the road as planned. She parked her truck behind the cruiser and turned off the engine. It was raining. She watched through the blur of her windshield as the sheriff walked toward her. The social workers had come with him. The two female workers were both older and seemed friendly. Skye invited them to sit in the cab of the truck as they explained their expectations of her interactions with the children. One was heavyset and the truck shifted as she slid along the seat to make room for the other, who was younger and more petite. The larger one told her that the parents had become progressively worse over the past three years. Originally, they seemed like a nice older farming couple, albeit a little eccentric, who couldn't have kids of their own. Recently, there had been attempts to discuss the hoarding in the house; the awareness of the animals was new. She told Skye that the dogs, to her knowledge, weren't bred to sell, *just more possessions*; and that the adopted children all came from one family. There won't be room inside the house to talk, she told Skye. She recommended that she *engage* the children, get them to assist her with the animals in the barn.

The three of them slid out of the truck and into the rain. The sheriff was already at the front door. Skye looked into the house at the frail-looking owners surrounded by their piled-to-the-ceiling newspapers, boxes and bags. A man, who looked to be about sixty, invited Skye into the kitchen, but it was hard for her to find a place to stand. One of the children appeared from the clutter, a thin girl of about twelve, cradling a puppy. Skye asked the girl if she could pet the puppy and if she could show her the other dogs in the barn. The child wouldn't let her touch the pup, but agreed to show her the barn. The two of them squeezed past the sheriff and the social workers. The parents remained silent. One of the workers suggested that the child put a coat on because of the rain; she ignored her and ran out the front door ahead of Skye.

The smell in the barn was horrific, and Skye was grateful for the cool, fresh air that the rain brought. She searched for the light switch and couldn't find one — the child said that it was broken anyway. Skye propped the barn doors open with stones. She looked over cage after broken cage of barking dogs, and the child ran from one to the other, dropping a handful of food on the floor of each. Some had water bowls and some had a little straw to keep them warm. One by one, Skye pushed her way through the odour of feces and urine and brought down each cage to carefully examine the animal inside. She found eye infections, dehydration, malocclusions, ear and parasitic infections. She worked her way through one row of stacked cages, then moved on to the next. Many of the dogs in the bottom cages were suffering from hypothermia — soaking wet from a turned-over water bowl in the cage above it, or urine. She knew she was going to find one of them dead by the smell even before she saw it, covered with maggots, lying in the back of its cage. Skye walked back to the house and interrupted the conversation — "I want towels, lots of them. Now," she said to the worker, not able to control the anger in her voice or bring herself to look at the parents. Then she saw one of the younger children playing on the dirty kitchen floor and she lowered her voice: "Let's keep the doggies nice and warm."

"You're stealing our dogs," the woman said to Skye's back as she walked out the door.

•

When Skye arrived home she took off her clothes and dropped them in a pile at the door. Knowing that Duncan would still be at school, she walked naked through the house, up to the second floor. She ran the hot water to the top of the tub and had a long, soapy bath, trying to erase the images of that barn and those dogs from her head. She put on her robe and walked down the stairs. In the kitchen, she found a large trash bag and walked to the front door with it in her hand. She put the clothes in the bag and set the bag outside the door in the rain that was still coming down. She went back to the kitchen and put on the kettle for tea. At the table she sighed, and relaxed her shoulders. She opened the drawer and took out her book: *Life Lessons for Duncan. Canis lupus familiaris*, she wrote.

The final dog to be tagged and carted out was a liver-coloured Springer male. About six months old, it was severely dehydrated and had an eye infection and open sores on both back legs. He cowered when Skye approached him. She talked to him and gave him a treat, wrapped him in a towel before putting him in a clean, dry cage. She carried him to the truck and was about to set the cage down when the man approached her and asked if he could say goodbye to his dog. *Don't see the harm*, Skye said. When the owner reached inside, the dog cowered and growled, moved back in the cage. When the owner picked him up by the scruff of his neck and held him, the dog wagged his tail and licked his master's face.

# KINCARDINE, 1997

Duncan sketched fast and didn't stop to question his logic or skill. His lines were chaotic and long, his images didn't make much sense to others — they were filled with swirls of light and vibrant images.

"If you try harder," his grade ten art teacher said. "your images will look more like real cows, cats and dogs, rather than these shaggy, mythical creatures."

# TORONTO, 2005

Skye always had good luck at Wonder Works on Harbord Street in Toronto. A small gift shop nestled close to the Women's Bookstore, it sold music, books, candles, sweet grass, cards, and other unique gifts, many of them having a spiritual element — tarot cards, the *I Ching* and *Daily Meditations for Women*. The environment was serene, and Skye always looked forward to her annual trip here to start her Christmas shopping. One of the staff was unpacking a box of bumper stickers, and Skye spotted this one immediately — a mauve peace sign against a yellow background with a few bumblebees flying around it: *Give Bees a Chance*, it read. The woman behind the counter smiled at Skye and reminded her that it was the anniversary of John Lennon's death.

"Oh my," said Skye, reaching across the counter, picking out three of the bumper stickers. "These will be perfect for my staff."

"What kind of work do you do?" the woman asked.

"I'm a veterinarian," Skye said, feeling a little self-conscious.

"How wonderful," the woman said looking down at her feet. "She'd be long dead if it wasn't for our vet."

Skye leaned across the counter and could see an old Pomeranian sleeping near the woman's feet.

"She must be very old," said Skye, "to be avoiding me like this. They usually have very active vocal chords."

"Oh yes," said the woman. "She should be long gone by now, but she keeps going and going."

Skye paid for her purchase and left the store. She walked down Harbord Street looking for her car. Rory had a running joke that he used to say whenever the opportunity presented itself.

"We're both Vets," he loved to tell. "She's a vet and so am I."

People would look puzzled, as most people in town knew that he worked with wood. "I'm a war veteran," he'd say. "Get it. Vet. Veteran. Veterinarian."

"They get it, Rory," Skye would say, amused and annoyed by his sense of humour.

•

Skye could never remember where she parked the car in the city. In Bruce County she could drive down back roads in all kinds of weather at all times of the day and night and never lose her direction. But the city was different. The grid pattern annoyed her; the buildings blocked her view of the stars. She turned onto Spadina Avenue and walked north. After a few minutes it began to snow and Skye worried about driving home in the storm the weatherman had predicted. She stopped at College and realized that she'd gone too far. She looked around, trying to get her bearings. In front of the Salvation Army, there was a line forming for the night's beds. Skye looked over the men with their sleeping bags and backpacks. A few of them were curled up on the sidewalk, passed out. One guy shouted at people who passed by without dropping change into the hat he held. Skye turned to walk in the other direction when it hit her. *Dear God Almighty, could it be?* That man looked like Magnus, only twenty years older and without teeth. She kept walking. She didn't look back to double-check. She didn't want him to see her. She pushed into the cold wind. She thought that she should turn back. Then she thought she should keep walking. She considered at least putting something in his hat, but didn't. She thought about how fastidious Magnus had always been about his teeth. She clutched her parcel to her chest and kept walking. As the snow got heavier, she considered staying in the city for the night. Duncan would be fine on his own for one night; he was a young man now. Skye was distracted beyond her thoughts about the storm and Duncan. She stopped and turned around. With the wind at her back she walked back up the street. She would find out if that man was Magnus. She would talk to him. She would point him in the right direction once and for all. By the time she got back to the Salvation Army, the lineup had disappeared. All the men had gone inside except for the two who were sleeping on the sidewalk near the corner. She walked to the door and peeked in. She couldn't see anything and was embarrassed when a staff member tapped against the window from inside and waved her away. *This isn't a circus,* Skye heard through the glass. She turned and suddenly remembered where she'd parked the car.

# KINCARDINE, 2008

Sarah Palin says she's just a normal small-town girl with God and family on her mind.

"What's the difference between a hockey mom and a pit bull?" she asks her adoring audience. The crowd waits for the answer to her riddle. They know it will be clever, a carefully crafted cuss-free dig against liberals, communists, and anti-Christians. Her timing is perfect.

"Lipstick," she says, and the Tea Party crowd goes wild.

*Leave the dogs out of this*, Skye says to the television.

She walks to the kitchen and sits down at the table thinking about Rocky. He's been gone well over ten years now and she still misses him. Yes, on one hand he was just a dog, a loyal pet; on the other, he took something of hers with him — life, spirit, willingness to live minute by minute in nature? Skye doesn't want to put too much into it, but she knows the importance of companionship. Aside from Siobhan, Duncan spends all of his time alone. Thank God for the teaching job, maybe he'll meet someone at work? Be an artist, she'd told him, but secure a paying job first. *Being practical hasn't gone out of fashion. Have you ever thought of becoming a teacher?*

She pulls out the drawer and reaches inside for *Life Lessons: Dog: Canis lupus familiaris*

## RED FOX

| Species | Vulpes vulpes |
|---|---|
| Phylum | Chordata |
| Order | Carnivora |
| Family | Canidae |
| Description | A rusty red, almost orange; a solitary hunter who feeds on rodents, rabbits and bugs. She's graceful looking with black on the backs of her ears and lower limbs. |
| Attributes | We all know how clever the fox is — but few of us are aware of how adaptable she is to her environment. |

### Life Lesson for Duncan

Your mother is always with you — for better or worse. Know that her spirit clings to you, feel her love.

# KINCARDINE, 2009

The back windows of Beans Bistro face Lake Huron. The restaurant is long and narrow with mismatched chairs and tables. The wood panelling is painted mint green. It has brick-patterned wallpaper, a 1970s fake fireplace, and laminate floors. The wall units contain a collection of tea and coffee pots, mugs, cups and photographs; computers and outdated VCRs sit on tacky coffee tables — like someone's 1980s basement apartment. From a bookstand next to his table, Duncan picks up a binder with a red plaid cover labelled "Scottish Trivia." It includes sections on food, humour, and faeries: Ashrays and Muckselavees. He's constantly reminded of Kincardine's Scottish heritage and traditions, but he's trying to forget about Scotland right now. He's also trying not to think about Skye, who's in the hospital because she's had pain in her chest and vertigo. *You have to pay attention, Grandma Skye*, he'd told her when he came home and found her resting with her head on the kitchen table. *This could be serious.*

*I've lived plenty*, she answered back.

Duncan puts down the binder. On one hand, her statement holds a lot of truth. On the other, he knows that Skye isn't ready to die. She's driven, still focussed on a goal that she keeps to herself, still holding some half-disclosed secret close to her heart. *There are things I should tell you*, she'll say. Or, *I brought this upon myself.*

He tries to concentrate on the task at hand, but it's difficult. It's early morning and the dream is still fresh in his mind. It's always the same: he's walking in a forest, it could be Africa or it could be Algonquin Park — sometimes the trees look deciduous, sometimes they're tropical. He comes to a clearing where there's a herd of elephants. He is astonished by their size and excited by the encounter. He is young, perhaps six or seven years old. In the dream, he walks toward the elephants. He wants to pet the baby that is standing between his mother's front legs. The mother elephant flaps her ears and he can feel her power. He stops. *Hello to you, Missus elephant*, he says. She stomps and trumpets. He's frightened by the sound, and by the sight of a bull elephant that seems to come out of nowhere. He can't move. The male elephant charges, the baby runs toward him and together they race through the forest. He hears crashing in the bushes behind him as the baby elephant passes and runs through the trees. There is silence in the forest, no sign of the bull elephant. He can hear the baby crying in the bushes. Suddenly the bull elephant appears again and he feels the weight of its massive foot on his throat. He can't breathe. This is where he always wakes up with a lump in his throat. This is when he remembers the time he swallowed the picture of his parents.

Duncan shakes his head and sips his coffee. He sketches images from his dream: the mother's massive grey ears and her baby's stumpy, wrinkled legs; the aggressive bull and his raised trunk; the circle of toppled trees. Maybe the frequency of the dream means that he needs a break? Maybe this time Skye's advice makes sense?

"You're a teacher, Duncan," she tells him. "You have the entire summer to go somewhere nice if you want. Maybe you'll meet someone nice?"

"I can't think of a better place than here in the summer," he tells her, and almost means what he says.

He's drawn the dream a thousand times, pencilled in every detail of the forest, including how tiny he looks against the advancing bull and details of its enormous foot like a grey boulder wedged across his throat. He puts down his pencil and looks around at the people in the bistro. Saturday breakfast is one of the busier times at Beans. He starts doing his assignment inside his head: woman with slicked-back black hair: Crow face. Woman with blonde hair and pointed nose: Dog face. Old man with sagging cheeks and bad teeth: Rat face. The guy with a face round as a moon, pockmarked skin and a tiny crater mouth: Owl face. Duncan always does every assignment that he gives his students. He cuts pictures from magazines. He writes words to go with the images, and then makes a sentence from the words. He draws people who look like their pets, and he uses computer software to give an elephant legs like a giraffe's à la Salvador Dalí. It usually starts off a little boring, but almost always, he comes up with something that he is proud to show his students.

The inspiration for the Edinburgh project came from the cover story of the *National Enquirer* at Fincher's store on Queen Street. There was a blurred photograph of a dirty, semi-naked boy with long scruffy hair, running through a forest. The boy looked back over his shoulder, frightened, as if he had never seen anything human before — especially not a photographer who just happened to have his camera equipment set up in the middle of the woods at the precise moment he ran by.

Duncan draws image after image. At first they are drawings that look pretty much like the boy in the photograph, then they get more detailed and take on a whimsical quality. After hours of rapid drawing, one image after another in a forest setting, the image of a more evocative Wolf Boy forms on the paper. He has sandy hair and brown eyes, and like himself, he wears glasses. He's tall and stands with his arms folded, looking out across a classroom. Behind him is a chalkboard where he writes: *I was raised by a pack of kind-hearted wolves.*

He gives himself large, hairy hands and long, muscular legs. He wears a loincloth like Tarzan's that doesn't completely cover his privates. Feeling slightly self-conscious, he looks around the room. Moon-face guy has gone and there's only one table with people at it on the other side of the room — Michael Watson, the dentist, and his wife, Gail. Duncan looks back down at his drawing and adds a few more details. Wolf Boy is hung, and like himself semi-hard — he's always horny these days and he just doesn't feel like running off to Toronto every weekend looking to meet someone. Duncan tries to imagine a mate for Wolf Boy — *Same Sex Animal* he calls him. This is getting stupid, he tells himself, but doesn't stop. The naked wolves wrestle in piles of leaves. The wolves share a dead rabbit. The wolves look up through dreamy eyes to a perfectly blue summer sky. He draws a howling wolf with arched back, ripped, with big arms and strong thighs. The young wolves look at the father wolf that has silently entered the den.

⁂

A few weeks later at Beans, Duncan draws Moira as a red fox. Not for any particular reason other than he thinks of foxes as the embodiment of soft, wise creatures. He draws the mother fox slick and mischievous; he rounds her shoulders and narrows her eyes. He adds streaks of orange and gold to her coat. He makes her ears pointed, cautiously alert. It's as natural for him to imagine his mother as a fox as he assumes it is for other teenagers to think of their mothers as the ones who cook the meals or get out of bed on dark winter mornings to drive them to hockey practice. He draws a rabbit in the fox's mouth; Duncan sees her as free and capable — a nurturer, the mother fox is a roaring red spirit.

*Tell me about her*, Duncan asked Skye, when he was a little boy.

*Your mother was beautiful*, Skye told him. *There was light in her eyes like a forest lake; shimmering gold and green.*

*Ah*, Duncan said, trying to take in the image. *Do you think you could show me the lake some time?*

Skye kissed him on the forehead. *Sure, sweet boy*, she said.

*And what about my dad; what did he look like?* Duncan asked, pulling away from her.

She sighed, crossed and uncrossed her legs. She put her elbow on the table and her chin in her hand.

*He was a little guy*, she said. *But built like an ox.*

*Oh*, said Duncan. *And were his eyes like an ox too?*

*No*, said Skye, sitting back in her chair and folding her arms across her chest. *Magnus's eyes are more like fire. Your father has heat and strength in him.*

It was Duncan's turn to fidget. He dropped his pencil. He stood up and sat down. Then he too put his elbow on the table, and his chin in his small hand.

*That's good, isn't it, Grandma Skye? That means he won't never die.*

✄

For their final exam, Duncan asked his grade ten class to alter an illustration from a children's book. They were to change the cover image into something new that meant something to them by using at least one of the techniques they'd learned that semester. They could turn a two-dimensional object into a three-dimensional; they could change the mood of the drawing; they could alter the point of view. They could use any medium that they wished — charcoal, oils, water colours. He had gone to the library and picked out twenty-two books; he stacked them on his desk in front of the classroom. These are in no real order, he told them, and asked Zach to pass the books around to his classmates.

"Yes!" said Cynthia. "I got *The Cat and the Bell.*"

"Gross," said Erica. "I got *The Goose That Laid the Golden Egg.*"

Phil gets *The Fox and the Crow*; and Pete gets *Beautiful Joe.*

"Good luck, Pete," Duncan said as he walked by his desk.

"*Good luck, Pete,*" he heard Erica mock him.

"Sir?" said Pete. "*Beautiful Joe* is a novel, not a children's book."

"I put that book into the pile because it's local. Everyone knows the story of the hard-luck dog from Meaford, and I want one of you to respond to the cover illustration. Look at that cover," Duncan said. "You can do a lot with that, Pete. I know you're capable."

Erica started to say something, but Duncan cut her off. "Nothing else from you, Erica, now focus. All of you," he said, raising his finger to his lips, "shhh…and good luck."

✄

Duncan finds this the most rewarding part of the year — seeing the progression in his students' art; watching how much they learned during the year. He sits with a plate of cookies and a pot of coffee grading the exams in his living room at home. So far, there are no big surprises. Cynthia's drawing is a carbon copy of the original book cover; nothing adventurous, but enough changes and advanced technique to keep her status as an *A* student. Erica's work is edgy with powerful, bold lines. Duncan puts his feet up on the sofa and looks out the window...a gorgeous late spring day, and soon he'll have time to work on his own art. The next two drawings are *C's* — in both cases, the students simply copied the existing illustration without incorporating anything new, with very little skill or originality. When he gets to Pete's drawing of *Beautiful Joe*, Duncan takes his feet off the table and sits up straight. He checks the name again at the bottom of the drawing and affirms that it is, in fact, Pete's. The story of Joe is one that most people in Bruce County know. The dog, part bull terrier and part fox terrier, had been horribly abused. His owner had starved and beat him; even cut off his tail and ears. The dog was rescued and when his story was told, it contributed to nationwide awareness of animal cruelty. His story inspired a novel, the first written from the animal's point of view. Pete had taken a rather romantic book cover image of the sad-faced dog with a bandana wrapped around his head tied at the top in a bow, and transformed it into something demonic — the points of the bow had been changed to horns, and the dog's quiet, brown eyes blazed red and orange. He foamed at the mouth and his sharp teeth were like a viper's. The whiskers were spikes and the nostrils flared wide. Beautiful Joe had scars on his face and a tattoo on his shoulder — *JOE* in a heart with an arrow through it.

❦

Pete had done everything that he was asked to do — he took an image and transformed it into something of his own. He incorporated all of the techniques he'd been taught through the year in Duncan's class. The drawing of Beautiful Joe was angry and disturbing, but definitely warranted an *A*. But Pete? Duncan debated all afternoon about calling the boy at home. His drawing was a dramatic departure from his usual art which tended to be poetic, almost boring. And beyond the art, Pete was becoming more withdrawn at school, and fearful. He finished grading the rest of the papers and picked up the phone.

"Is Pete there?" he asked, when the father answered.

It took a long time for Pete to come to the phone, and Duncan began to have regrets about his decision to call.

"Hello?" said a worried voice.

"Hi, Pete," Duncan said, trying to sound upbeat. "This is Mister Johnson."

"Hi, sir," he said.

"Well," said Duncan, pausing because he could hear a loud voice in the background: *It better not be that fruitcake teacher.* "I just called to congratulate you. You got an *A* on your exam."

"Thank you, sir," said Pete, hanging up.

※

Self-confidence hadn't always been his strength. As a teenager Duncan had been called *weird* and *faggot* and his response had always been to withdraw. As a teacher he could be different, model confidence to his students.

"It's not all feelings," Skye told him. "You have emotions *and* a brain, so use them both. Let that boy's father know that someone has their eye on the situation."

He was angry about the father's *fruitcake* comment and concerned about the boy; but, at first, Duncan couldn't bring himself to say anything to the father. Pete had transformed a gentle illustration into something disturbing. There was violence in his drawing, and although Duncan wasn't a psychology major, he knew what was hidden in the jagged lines and dark tones.

As the week went on and he thought about things more, Duncan accepted that he had a responsibility to check things out. *It better not be that fruitcake teacher*, Duncan heard in the background. *Thank you, sir*, Pete had said. There was shaking in his voice.

"But I don't have enough to go on," he told Skye.

"You're pulling my leg," she said. "*That fruitcake teacher?*"

"I think that's what I heard him say," Duncan said. "The father was in the background, I couldn't hear too well."

"You can ignore what's in front of you, Duncan Johnson. Or," Skye said, throwing the gold silk cover onto the kitchen table, "you can step into the problem — march up the street and have the conversation that needs to be had with that father."

"Where did you find this thing?" Duncan asked her.

"The same place it has been for the last twenty-some odd years...at the foot of your bed."

Duncan had never known any other way of making his bed. The gold blanket was folded and placed at the foot of it for as long as he could remember. It was there like the bed post or chest of drawers — nothing significant, part of the furniture.

"Why are you dragging this old piece of silk into this conversation?" he asked.

"Because it comes with good intentions. It was sent from Scotland with the spirit of good will. It was sent to your mother to remind her that she comes from a long line of fighters."

Duncan picked up the silk cloth and folded it in two, and then two again. He kept folding it until it was the size of a small, gold pillow. He carried it up the stairs to his bedroom and put it on his bed. He put his head on it and slept and dreamt of his mother as a gold fox and his father as a dragon. He dreamt that he was flying over Loch Dunvegan, and when he woke in the morning and looked out his window he recognized the same clouds from his dream — wispy and blue as the ones he dreamt over Skye.

That Saturday morning, Duncan drove to the grocery store and bought a cake. He set it down on the passenger seat of the car. He drove over to the house where Pete lived with his parents and brothers. He'd called ahead and arranged a time with the mother. The house looked like every other bungalow on the street, perhaps a little more worn down than some. The grass had been cut and there were red geraniums planted along the sidewalk. Duncan walked up to the door with the cake in a bag by his side.

It was Pete who answered the door, holding back a small dog by its collar. It looked like a Jack Russell or maybe a mix of Russell and Doberman. It had short legs like a terrier, but the pointed ears and long jaw of a Doberman.

"He's harmless," said Pete. "Sit, Spinner."

"We got him from the shelter," the mother said, stepping up behind her son. "He's nervous with strangers."

It hadn't occurred to Duncan until that instant that Pete's drawing might be based on a real-life animal. The dog growled at him, then wagged his stump of a tail. The three of them walked into the living room, the dog jumping up against Duncan, sniffing the bag with the cake in it. The father didn't bother to get up from his La-Z-Boy. Six or seven of Pete's drawings were framed on a wall behind him, including the one of Beautiful Joe that Duncan had sent to him in the mail with a note. *We should talk about this,* he wrote.

"May I put that somewhere for you?" the mother asked, pointing to the bag that Duncan was holding away from the barking dog.

"Sorry," he said. "I almost forgot. I brought a cake."

"Thank you," said the mother, taking the bag from his hand. "You shouldn't have. Would you like a coffee or a glass of juice?"

"No, thank you," said Duncan, as Pete and his mother left the room. The small dog spun in circles, jumping up and down behind them.

"What am I?" shouted the father. "I wouldn't mind a coffee."

Duncan stood for what seemed like an eternity, before the man waved him to the sofa.

"Take a load off your feet," he said. "What brings you here to our humble abode on a Saturday?"

"Your house is very nice," said Duncan, aware that his voice was cracking.

"Oh, I'm sure you have a nicer place," he said. "You types always do."

"I live with my grandmother," said Duncan.

"Oh yes," said the father. "The famous Skye Rayburn. She never did too much for Spinner's nerves."

"What do you mean *you types*?" asked Duncan, his heart pounding hard and his hands shaking. But before the man could answer, the dog raced back into the room, Pete and his mother behind him.

"Look at what Mister Johnson brought," she said, holding out the cake on a tray. "A lovely fruitcake. It's a fruitcake, I mean," the mother continued, stumbling for words. "Mister Johnson brought us a cake."

"Call it what it is," said the father, looking at Duncan, "a strange, soppy fruitcake."

Duncan struggled for composure and the right language, but nothing seemed to go right. He tried to look confident for Pete and the mother.

"That's not acceptable," he said, as the father reached down for the lever on the side of the La-Z-Boy.

"That kind of language is hurtful," Duncan continued, as the father stood two inches from his face.

"Get out of my house," he said.

Duncan could smell coffee and cigarettes on his breath, and stepped back a few inches before trying to speak again.

"Now!" the father said, raising his voice.

※

"How did it go?" Skye asked when he walked through the door.

"Bad," Duncan said, noticing two plates and two forks on the kitchen table. "I sounded like an awkward social worker. I stuttered and shook. I was a complete wimp."

"But you did it, Duncan," Skye said, touching his arm. "You stepped up to the problem with your shoulders back and head held high."

# PART VI

# TORONTO, 2010

The dumpster behind Rabba Foods on Queen's Quay is best for unopened bread. Sometimes there are leftovers from the takeout counter, and sometimes they throw out fruit and vegetables if they have brown spots. It's going to be a hot day; already the dumpster stinks real bad. Magnus crawls inside and looks through bags of rotting food; he has to push back an old desk to reach a dented tin of peaches. He throws the tin onto the pavement and crawls out after it. Magnus smashes it against the sidewalk and claws out the perfectly good peaches. He throws the empty tin back into the dumpster, wipes his sticky fingers on his pants, and walks around to the front of the store where he sits with his empty Starbucks cup in front of him. He's not allowed to ask for money from the customers there anymore, but he knows that he can get an empty cup from the trash. He used to hold his hand out, but he learned quickly that people didn't want to touch him when they gave him change. It's not a good day for coin. The weather's too nice and only a few people walk by. No one drops a cent in his hat when it's warm and sunny — he needs rain or a good snowstorm for that. Most days he stays close to the silos, but today Magnus decides to go to Yonge Street. The Eaton Centre is good for tourists. There's also a beer store on the way that will serve him.

In front of Sears there's a teenage boy who has a sign that says Houdini of the Chicken House. It's the Dundas Square entrance and thousands of people rush past. Magnus sits on the sidewalk leaning against a sign post. He won't put his hat down while the kid's here; there are rules that street people respect. He'll go to the Queen Street side, sit close to the revolving doors. As he gets up to leave, the boy spins a live chicken over his head three times, sets the bird down on the concrete.

"Gather 'round," he shouts. "I can make this genius bird talk."

The boy, probably the same age Duncan is now, walks around the chicken that keeps falling as if it has rubber legs.

"Go ahead," he says to a gathering crowd. "Ask her any question you want."

The boy draws the letters of the alphabet in a circle around the staggering bird. Magnus starts to leave, but is drawn back by the boy's voice.

"Any question for the chicken?" the boy yells to the crowd. "Go ahead. Ask her and she'll spell out her answer using these letters."

"What's your name, chicken?" a middle-aged man in a grey suit yells, while the rest of the crowd laughs.

"The chicken will tell you her name in good time," says the boy holding out a pink Frisbee. "But first, your wager."

The crowd boos and people start to walk away.

"Twenty bucks for her name," says the business guy, dropping two tens into the Frisbee.

The chicken, regaining her strength, starts to wander. The boy picks her up and waves her, three more times, in a circle above his head.

"Anyone else?" he asks, setting the chicken back down on the sidewalk. "She can take up to three questions at a time."

Two teenage girls in silver shoes and short skirts drop coins into the Frisbee.

"We both have the same question," one of the girls says. "Does that count as one?"

"Of course one question counts as one," the boy says. "Another question from the crowd?"

"Hey, you don't even know our question yet," the girl says. "We want to know if Lady Gaga is really a boy."

"Yeah, what about my question?" says the grey suit guy. "I gave you twenty bucks!"

"Your questions will be answered," says Houdini of the Hen House, "but one last question before we get our chicken talking."

It feels like a hundred degrees out. There's no shade on the sidewalk, and Magnus is getting thirsty. He has to get moving if he's going to make any money.

"Where's your licence?" asks a strong voice from the back of the crowd.

"Speak up," says the boy. "Did you ask something back there?"

"Where's your busker's licence?" asks a man holding up a badge as he shoves through the crowd.

"I'm not a busker," says the boy, picking up the chicken, as the crowd starts to move away.

The guy with the badge picks up the Frisbee with the money in it. Magnus doesn't move. He leans against a lamppost, watching from a safe distance.

"I want my twenty bucks," says the businessman, "or else the bird to answer my question."

"Her name is Thursday," says the boy.

"Not you, idiot," the man says. "You said that the chicken could talk."

"Pardon me," says the man with the badge. "You want the chicken to talk?"

The businessman walks away, calling the boy names, as the last of the crowd moves on.

"Good work," says the boy to the man with the badge once everyone has gone.

"Good work to you too, young lady," the man says, patting the hen on the head, feeding her a handful of grain. He gives the boy the Frisbee without the money in it, and they both leave the corner with the chicken tucked under the boy's arm.

# KINCARDINE, 2010

Duncan wrote *Faces of Fear/ Faces of Joy* on the chalkboard.

"This assignment has four main components," he told his grade eleven art class.

He wrote a giant number 1 on the board.

"Part one involves keeping a sketchbook," he said.

The students let out a collective groan. They always groaned, even if it was something they liked.

"I want you to use the internet, magazines and photographs, to collect a range of facial expressions. Once you have the images you want," he said, "brainstorm words that you associate with the picture. Then, using charcoal, draw two of them."

"What's brainstorm mean?" Cynthia asked. Cynthia wanted to get it right, she was always the first to ask for clarification.

"What do you think brainstorm is?" he said back.

"Like free association," she said.

"Exactly," said Duncan. "Use whatever word comes into your head when you look at the picture."

Duncan writes a large 2 on the board.

"The second part," he said, "will be a little more challenging."

The students groaned again, but laughed at their own collective response. Duncan felt the energy shift in the room from worry to excitement. He decided to prolong the good energy.

"Do any of you have a guess what the second part of this will be?" he asked.

"Something more kinda crazy," said Erica, without raising her hand or looking up from her desk.

"Crazy like what?" Duncan asked Pete, who seemed to have undergone a major transformation between grade ten and eleven. His soft qualities had disappeared and his shyness had been replaced by aggression. "What do you think Erica's getting at?"

"Crazy-weird," he said, not looking up from his desk.

"Anything else?" Duncan asked the room, disturbed by Pete's tone.

"I know," said Zach. "Something about animals."

"Oh, like that's a surprise," said Erica, making the others laugh.

"It is and it isn't," said Duncan. "I want you to go to the internet and find an image of an animal and change the animal face to look like a human's. Or ..." he says, "...find the image of a human and change it into an animal. Create something unusual, something that will surprise people."

First they moaned. Then they all started talking at once.

"Can you give an example?" asked Cynthia.

"Perhaps someone with dark hair, a long nose and thin face, could become a crow," Duncan explained.

"Cool," said Erica.

"How are we supposed to do that?" asked Zach.

"Use software," Duncan explained. "The librarian can help you out."

"Duh," said Phil. "Or a photocopier. Or friggin' draw it."

"Whoa," said Duncan. "There's no *duh* in my classroom, we're in this together. There are two more parts."

"This is too hard," said a voice from the back row.

Duncan faced the chalkboard again, wrote a 3. "This is not too hard," he said. "You're all up to this. The third part," he began, "is due after the Christmas break. It involves using both sides of your brain. I want you to write a sentence under each image. A complete sentence about the image using the words that you brainstormed. One sentence. No more. No less."

The grunts and groans got worse. A few of the students slammed their notebooks shut.

"Who has read *The Raven*? Who grew up with *The Cat in the Hat*? Who's ever seen a Tim Burton movie ...?"

He didn't need to go any further. "He's way cool," Erica said.

They all followed Erica's lead. Duncan knew he'd get them with Tim Burton.

"Use your art and use your brain to start something spectacular. You're all capable of genius."

"Can we do a brainstorm?" Cynthia asked. "Can you show us?"

Duncan held up a photograph of a crow and wrote the word CROW on the board and circled it. "What do you think of when you see this crow? Or see this word?"

Silence. None of the students were willing to take a risk. Duncan drew a line from the word crow and wrote: BLACK.

"What else?" he asked.

"Feathers like ink," said Cynthia.

"Excellent."

"Pellet eyes," said Erica.

"Perfect."

But just as quickly as the exercise began, it stopped. The students seemed out of ideas.

"Feet pie," Duncan wrote.

"Feet pie?" said Phil. "Gross."

Duncan stopped. He put the chalk down and turned to face the class.

"You get the drift," he said. "Just write. Think about your image and write."

"*Feet pie*," said Cynthia, scrunching her face.

"Strange," said Pete, sounding just like his father, "weird assignment."

# TORONTO, 2010

Magnus finished the mickey and bought another and then he started to walk back to the Malting Silos. It was raining and his feet were numb and he needed to go to the bathroom. He pulled down his pants and used a piece of newspaper to clean himself. He tried to pull his pants back up, but slipped in the mud. In his head he could see himself falling, but couldn't make his body stop. In his mind he knew that he should stand up, but he couldn't. He felt blood trickle down the side of his face; he tried to keep his eyes open. The rain came down harder; he covered his face with his sleeve.

# KINCARDINE, 2008

Skye pushed back the blankets and sat on the edge of the bed. She got the blood flowing by pressing her feet two or three times into the floor. She pulled her walker close to the bed, tested its steadiness, slowly lifted herself up. She inhaled deeply because it all took strength and conviction. She moved the walker, inch by inch, toward the light of the bathroom door. She hung on to the towel rack with both hands and turned herself around. She let go with one hand and removed the sleeve of her housecoat. Then she did the same on the other side. She let it drop to the floor and kicked it aside. Still hanging on with one hand, she removed the Velcro on the right side and then the left; the wet Depend fell to the floor. She kicked that aside too. Both hands back on the towel rack, she lowered herself onto the toilet. She was itchy and dry, and no urine came out. Joy, joy, joy, she mocked herself. I got joy, joy, joy, joy down in my heart. She raised herself up and heard the towel rack crack as she pulled. On the laundry hamper there was a stack of disposable diapers; she took one off the top and worked it between her legs. She bent slowly to reach her housecoat, put it on, one arm at a time. All her things had been moved to the main floor of the house now; she couldn't remember the last time she'd seen the upstairs.

Light poured in from the window above the kitchen sink and she heard the crows before she saw a large one flutter up into the weeping ash. Caw caw. Caw caw. There's nothing as wonderful as the call of a crow through her kitchen window on a summer morning. The yard had always been her favourite part of the house on Princes Street. A slight rolling hill in the back and room enough for six large maples along the side. The McKendricks built the house, she was told. There's a whole pile of them down at the cemetery.

"What are you fellows yapping about?" she said to the crows. "Caw caw yourself." *Genus: Corvus*, she made a mental note.

Rory loved the crows and fed them. The neighbours will hate you for that, she told him. "Heckle and Jeckle need to eat too," he said, throwing the scraps from his breakfast plate across the yard, along with a slice of toast. He stole those names from the cartoon that used to be on television. He had other names too.

"That one's Lady Macbeth," he'd say about the large crow causing a scene by flapping her wings, strutting across the yard as she cawed. "And that's our fine Mister Brodie," he'd say, pointing to a stout little crow with short black legs and a wings like an old Deacon's cap. "He's a sneaky one, he'll rob ya blind when your back is turned."

When Duncan was very young he was afraid of crows.

"They don't run away when I chase them."

"Well then perhaps you don't want to chase them," she'd say back.

"But they make that awful noise and they're big and they're not even afraid of Tom."

Tom was the feral cat who wandered the neighbourhood. He looked like a retired boxer with a beat-up face and only one ear. Tom was one of the few strays who could survive a Kincardine winter, and Duncan was right, the crows seemed to torment him rather than fear him.

"Good on them," she said. "Tom rules this neighbourhood as it is."

"But they watch me too," Duncan said. "They stare at me when I'm in the yard and they holler when I go by."

"Did you ever think that maybe they are watching out for you?" she said. "Crows are sentinels. They know this is our house. They are better guards than even Rocky was."

"Really?"

"Yes," said Skye.

"Like a father would?"

"I suppose," Skye said, unsettled by the comment.

# TORONTO, 2008

Magnus found the Malting Silos on the internet. He'd spent most of his time at the library until they kicked him out. *No drinking in here. No drinking and that smell bothers our regular patrons*, the librarian said.

Magnus knew better than to ask what she meant by *regular patrons*. He bent over to pick up his duffle bag as he pushed his chair away from the computer but changed in his mind.

"I don't think you should come back tomorrow," the security guard with the nose-piercing told him. "There's overcrowding because of the renovations," she said, pointing to the sheets of plastic hanging from the cornered-off area where they were drilling into the ceiling.

Magnus nodded his head in agreement and pointed at the computer screen. "Would you mind printing this off for me?"

She started to open her mouth, but didn't speak. Magnus smiled, showing her a little of his younger, more presentable self.

"Just one page," she said, looking at the monitor with a picture of the Canada Malting Silo.

"My new home," he said, when she handed him the page. "I'll be there just after dark."

Magnus had found a site: *Forbidden Places*. The bloggers were specific on how to get into the abandoned building. They even provided details of places not to go and a warning that people who enter risk their lives.

He'd been kicked out of Seaton House and he'd been kicked out of the Harbour Light. He'd been kicked out of every place he'd ever lived, for that matter, even the rooming house where he'd lived for the first two years after he left Kincardine.

"How could you?" asked the woman he brought home from Jillies. "How could you leave your kid?" Then, as she put on her skirt and shoes: "Especially after killin' your wife. Accident or no accident, it's the same thing if you did something stupid."

The summers weren't as bad, but Magnus was running out of places to stay at night. The east side of Toronto was becoming condo hell, and he read in the paper that the neighbourhood committees wanted the shelters and strip joints shut down.

Screw you all, he said, waving the picture of the Malting Silos at the clouds as he staggered down Yonge Street. He walked over to Roy Thomson Hall and sat on the Canada's Walk of Fame next to Shania Twain's star. He got about four dollars in his hat until he was asked to leave. He walked into the liquor store on Queen's Quay, then he sat on a bench in the Music Garden. He felt sick and it had started to snow. He walked along the pier to the Harbourfront Community Centre. On the sidewalk in front of the building he read words etched in stone:

I STILL DISTINCTLY REMEMBER
WHEN I FIRST ENTERED THE BEAUTIFUL BASIN
BENEATH THE LUXURIANT FOLIAGE
THE BAY AND NEIGHBOURING MARSHES
WERE THE HAUNTS OF IMMENSE COVEYS OF WILD FOWL
THE GROUND
FOR THE FUTURE METROPOLIS OF UPPER CANADA WAS FIXED

# TORONTO, 2008

Skye took a bus to London and a train from there to Toronto. She started with Seaton House men's shelter. She showed pictures and described what she could of him to the staff and the men living there. They gave her permission to sit at the entrance and wait. She wasn't allowed in, but she could ask anyone who came through the door of the shelter. Then, after about four hours, a dirty drunk man smelling of urine said in no uncertain terms, he's banned from here, he goes to Fred Victor now.

She took a taxi to the Fred Victor Mission and didn't have luck there either.

"He's kicked out of here," said a staff member. "We're not allowed to break confidentiality," he whispered. "But I've heard he spends most days at the Reference Library on Yonge Street."

The taxi ride up to the library didn't take long, but Skye was feeling hopeless. The woman at the information desk recognized him right away.

"Yes," she finally said, pointing at the photo of Magnus and Moira taken on their wedding day. "That's the short one we call Shaky. He was married?" Then catching herself and the expression on Skye's face, added, "But he can't help himself though, I'm sure."

"Have you seen him?" asked Skye, feeling hopeful.

"The last time he came in here he'd asked to use the photocopier. He had a picture of the Canada Malting Silos down by the lake. He's probably living in there. Yech…" she said, "…with rats and fleas and pigeons…"

"You're a life saver," said Skye. "Thank you."

"You're not going there? There's a fence and it's very dangerous."

"You must think I'm some silly old lady," she replied.

But outside, she crossed Yonge Street at the Bloor light. She stood on the west side of the street and flagged the first southbound taxi that came along.

She crawled under a fence, stumbled over bricks and rock; step by step, she inched her way along the waterfront to the abandoned Malting Silos. She carried the blue pillowcase in front of her with the money, beer, gold cover and the photographs of Duncan. Up close, the old building seemed more dilapidated than from far away; the moonlight, however, made them more beautiful. Skye walked close to the concrete wall until she found a rusty door that, much to her surprise, was unlocked. She hadn't given much thought to what she would do if the entrance were sealed; she'd just assumed that the homeless people rumoured to live there must get in somehow. Inside, she was overcome by the stench of damp and rot, but once her eyes adjusted to the dark, she walked forward, step by step, pulling the bag, calling his name. "Magnus," she whispered. And, as her courage grew: "Magnus, it's Skye," she shouted. When she encountered a knotted rope hanging from an iron stairwell, her heart nearly stopped — she was certain that someone may have used it for hanging themselves; then she'd realized that it was used to climb up to the higher levels. The graffiti on the walls was unnerving — skull heads and swastikas; strange writing, a secret language comprising dashes and swirls of spray paint. The building echoed — a faraway pebble bouncing off tin; bird flutter high up. On the ground there were candy wrappers, tins and bottles mixed in with peeled paint and crumbled brick. There were large mixing vats, chutes for the grains, and an old mattress. Skye heard rats squeaking and, occasionally, from the corner of her eye, she saw one scurrying under a ledge or sliding through a crack in the wall. On the mattress there was a strange pile that, at first, she thought could be a person.

"Magnus," she called. "It's Skye."

As she moved closer she could see that it was a mound of teddy bears, some with the stuffing pulled out, others with arms and legs missing, one of them with its glass eye hanging by a thread. A chill went through her and the wind blew through the walls and the broken windows. She felt as though she would die of fear. *What are you doing, you old fool*, she said to herself, and she turned around to leave when she saw him, like a ghostly child, standing in the dark.

"Magnus," she said. "Magnus Johnson?"

At first he didn't move, and she wondered if in fact she was seeing an apparition. She stepped closer and saw that his blond hair was long and matted, grey now, like his beard. His face was weathered and dirty, but those blue eyes were undeniably his.

"Don't be afraid," she'd said. "It's only old Skye, here to bring you home."

Skye was tired but couldn't see where she could possibly sit in the dirty chaos. She inched her way over to the mattress littered with bears. She reached into the bag and pulled out two beers. He took one of the bottles from her, and she tried to relax.

"I wouldn't sit on that," said Magnus, handing her an empty milk crate.

"You can talk?" she said, immediately regretting the tone in her voice.

"I'm homeless, not stupid."

"It's just that…well, you don't look too well."

"I'm fine, Skye," he said, reaching for the other beer.

"That's mine," she said. "One each."

"Old age has loosened you up," he said, twisting off the cap and passing it to her.

"I guess I really don't want it," she said, passing the bottle back. "I thought it might be something to break the ice."

"That's the Skye I remember, always a plan."

"Listen." She looked to a noise she'd heard on the catwalk above her. "I didn't come here to fight."

"Oh?"

"I brought you this." She passed him the blue bag. "Your son is a smart young man now."

Magnus wouldn't take the bag from her. He got up.

"I stink, Skye. I can't remember the last time I had a bath. I don't own a comb or a toothbrush anymore."

"Clearly," said Skye. "You're not that far gone that you couldn't come home?"

"Home!" Magnus laughed.

"Why not," said Skye. "Your son needs you."

"It's too late. I'm leaving, and if you were smart, you'd come too." He motioned his head up to the rafters where she'd heard the noises earlier, reached out his hand to help her to her feet.

She hadn't meant to hurt his feelings, the action came spontaneously, but when she let go of his hand and rubbed his dirt onto her sweater, she could see hurt in his eyes that reminded her of a younger, prouder Magnus.

"I'm old now," she said. "You might want to know what he looks like." She handed him the bag again. "He should have some family in his life when I'm gone."

He ignored her and walked away. She set the bag on the filthy mattress and anchored it in one corner with one of the stuffed bears.

"I'll leave it here," she said, not sure if he heard her. "Duncan has kept your wedding picture on his bedside table his entire life… I've put a copy in the bag."

There was a noise above. Skye looked up to the broken windows, then moved as quickly as she could in the direction of the door where she'd come into the building.

●

Magnus watched Skye get into a taxi on Queen's Quay, then he walked along the streetcar tracks and up Simcoe Street to his panhandling spot in front of Roy Thomson Hall. Sometimes he sat in front of Maurice Richard's star, and sometimes he sat in front of Denys Arcand's, but that day he sat in front of Jim Carrey's. Canada's Walk of Fame brings tourists, and tourists bring change and sometimes bills. He sat and waited with no strength for begging, but he wanted enough to get the biggest bottle of Lauder's he could carry. After four or five hours he walked back to the Silos with the bottle in his hand.

He knew every brick and pebble on the ground, the sound of birds and the sound of trouble, as when someone is lurking. Black Hood Guy was standing by the bed where Skye had dropped the bag.

"That's mine," Magnus said. "Put that bag down."

Black Hood dropped the bag and climbed up the rope to the catwalk. It was hard for him to climb because one of his hands clenched something he'd grabbed from Skye's bag. Magnus inched through the dark to the mattress. He sat and rifled through the bag. *That's a lot of pictures,* he'd said to her, looking at the stuffed blue pillowcase. *There's something else,* she said. *Money to get you started again.*

I don't want your charity, he told her, but now he was curious.

He reached into the bag and was pricked by something sharp at the bottom. He pulled out a kind of animal's claw made into a brooch or something with a purple tone on the end of it. Bigger than a rabbit's foot. Maybe a grouse claw, with a note attached by a thread. *This brooch is the very pin Rory and I used to etch our initials into the walls at Summerhall. Keep it and remember how useless guilt is. Death takes what it wants. Rory is gone. Moira is gone. Go find your son. I plead with you, Magnus, guilt is a bottomless snake; take this money and find a decent place to live. And this piece of jewellery means more than the money — Duncan will be waiting for you to return it.*

Magnus looked over to the knotted rope, still swinging in the dark. He picked up the picture of his son — the same eyes as his mother's, a handsome boy, but he also saw himself. The worried expression, the tentative smile that knows a cloud can cross over the sun with the blink of an eye.

Magnus tore up the picture and dropped to his knees. He thought for a second about climbing the rope, chasing down Black Hood Guy, but he didn't. Instead, he curled up on the concrete floor, the bottle of Lauder's clutched in one dirty fist, the torn photograph in the other. He thought about Moira's eyes; how he closed them himself, after the truck smashed through the car and took her, carried her spirit over the snow and ice.

# TORONTO, 2010

He had to get to his feet. Magnus knew that if he didn't stand and move that he would die. He'd promised Skye to deliver a message to Duncan. *Love yourself*, she'd said. *Love someone else — no rules but that.*

At first Magnus had told her that he was no authority on love and probably not the best person to pass on her message, but Skye had insisted. *You loved Moira. You loved Moira with every inch of your body and I could tell that. And when your son was born you loved him too and you were the proudest man in Kincardine. Enough of this, Magnus!* Skye said, throwing the bag down on the mattress. *You've had enough self-loathing for twenty lifetimes!*

*Maybe I'll do it*, he said, but Skye wouldn't take *maybe* as an answer. *I'm not leaving until you say you'll pull yourself together and do the right thing for your son.* She sat on the filthy mattress with her arms folded, looking up at something stirring above her on the catwalk.

*Okay*, he said, eventually. And when he asked her for five dollars, she looked at the bag that she'd thrown down and inched away through the dark.

Magnus stretched one leg out and then the other. He tried to sit up and pull up his pants at the same time. He needed a drink because the dry heaves were ripping apart his gut. He knew he needed to see a doctor because of the blood on his face and the colour of his fingers, he knew that last time they almost had to cut them off.

*The only obstacle here is yourself*, Skye had told him that day in the Malting Silos.

•

Magnus woke up in the hospital. His body ached and his skin itched.

"You're lucky to be alive, Mister S," a female voice said.

Magnus recognized the face and the gentle voice. He couldn't speak and didn't feel like it even if he could.

"They found you outside of the Malting Silos," she said.

It was Jo from the outreach van. Almost every single night for the last two years she'd shown up at his spot on the sidewalk with a blanket and a sandwich.

"You're going to get a star of your own on this walk," she'd told him once. "No, seriously," she said. "You're a pretty amazing guy."

And she meant it. She wasn't just teasing him, she had a big heart, that girl, and he knew it. She said her name was Jo Lynn, but that he could call her Jo. "What's your name?" she asked. It was cold that day and Magnus had dug his hands deeper into his pockets. He pricked himself on Skye's brooch again and didn't hesitate with his answer.

"Call me Screw," he'd said. "Short for Screw Up."

"How about Mister S?" she'd said.

Magnus reached under the sheets to feel if he was entirely naked.

"Bedbugs, Mister S," she said. "They took your clothes."

Weeks would go by where he wouldn't remember a thing. He'd wake up in the back of an ambulance or in a bed at a shelter. Sometimes he would make it back to the Silos and wake up holding his bottle of Lauder's, or one of Black Hood's headless bears. Once, there was a rat eating vomit by his head.

"I need my coat," he said.

"They'll give you a new one when you're discharged," Jo said. "I'll make sure."

"I need that one," he yelled. "There's something in the pocket."

"Shhh," said Jo. "I'll find the coat, but don't draw too much attention to yourself; the psych nurse will come back here and give you enough medication to put you out for a week."

"That wouldn't be such a bad thing," he said, turning his face to the wall.

# PART VII

# EDINBURGH, 1945

There wasn't much room to manoeuvre, but Rory led the way out of the washroom. He was the first to step out of the stall and make his way through the dark into the cloakroom area; the first to encounter the chair pushed aside, and the watchman with his note pad and threats.

"Please," Skye had pleaded with tears covering her face. "Please."

"We haven't committed a crime," Rory said.

Rory bent to pick up his coat and her scarf. He started to push past the watchman when another entered the room.

"This wouldn't go over too well at the Vannan estate," the second man said. He was stocky, with a big red moustache. He smelled of smoke.

Skye recognized him. He was the watchman who winked at her the day she arrived at Summerhall. The one some of the other girls bought cigarettes from.

"And your disrespect isn't going too well with her fiancé," Rory said, stepping forward.

"Won't you look at this," the second watchman said to the first, hiding something behind his back, "a big-mouthed soldier."

"Let's go," said Skye. "Excuse us," she said, trying to squeeze by the two men.

"Not so fast there," said the second watchman. "We need to see what our beautiful Vannan girl is hiding under her coat."

"You'll go to prison for the rest of your bloody lives," Rory said, taking a swing at the first watchman, who ducked his punch with little effort.

"Neither of us is going to jail," the second guy said, picking up Skye's bra and stockings from the floor. "We know what deed has been done here tonight. Now just sit down over there in the corner," he said, waving a pistol, "and keep your mouth shut, whilst we have a word with our girl here."

•

The watchmen wanted money, not her body.

"This isn't blackmail," the first one said. "It's just this one time, and we'll leave all this behind us."

"It's her parents who have money," Rory said, facing the wall, as instructed. "Not her."

"But she can get it," shouted the second watchman. And with that, his guard persona shifted to something softer. Lowering his voice, he added: "We want to go to New York."

"Skyscrapers," said the other.

"Good grief," said Rory, standing and turning to face them; noticing that they were practically holding hands, added, "They're queer as a pair of Canada geese."

"Watch what you say," said the second, waving the gun. "I'm a married man. Get back on your knees. We're not fooling around. You *will* get the money," he said to Skye. "You *will* cooperate," he said, pushing her to the ground next to Rory.

•

It was the thought of having to face her mother with some convoluted lie in order to get the money that caused Skye to sob.

"Honestly, Miss Vannan," the first watchman said. "We're not bad people. Just desperate to get to America."

"How much?" said Rory, standing and stepping closer.

"Back to your corner," said the second watchman, waving the pistol. "I know how to use this. I know about what's done to men like us in war."

"I'll try," said Skye. "How much?"

"One thousand pounds," said the second one.

"I couldn't possibly ask my parents for that kind of money without telling them what it's for," said Skye.

"Well, then take it," said the first one.

"Yes," said the second, standing closer to him. "Take it from them then."

Rory turned around and faced them. The men didn't object this time, so he stood and walked over to Skye and took her hand. He winked at her and she understood that she had to tell them whatever they wanted to hear.

"When do you need it?" she asked.

The two men looked at one another. They seemed puzzled, but the second one made the decision. "By Friday," he said. "Meet us in front of the Roxburghe Hotel on Charlotte Square."

They were allowed to gather their things and leave, but not without a final humiliation. "This would not go over too well," the second man said, handing her back her undergarments.

This time Skye winked at Rory. She could see his fist clench and his face darken with anger. "Thank you for sparing me that disgrace," she said, taking Rory's hand.

When they reached the front door of the building, Rory told her that they had no choice but to go to the police.

"It's blackmail," he'd said. "It will never end. Besides, we have something on them. I know they're queer and there are ways of finding out."

"No," said Skye. "Two wrongs don't make a right. I'll take the money from my dowry."

"You have a dowry?" Rory asked, genuinely surprised.

"Of course I have a dowry," she said. "What did you think?"

Rory told her that he hadn't given it much thought one way or the other. Then he went silent. They walked through the street past people staggering from the pubs after too much drink. He held her hand, and at one point, squeezed it tight. "I can make you happy."

"Of course you'll make me happy," she answered, not completely certain if she believed her own words. "A tall, handsome man like you…a soldier…a kind soul with a builder's hands," she said. She stopped and kissed his fingers. "I couldn't be more proud to be with someone like you."

They held one another in the street. She knew their life together had started; she felt it in the pit of her stomach.

•

Skye and Rory met the two security guards in front of the Roxburghe Hotel on Charlotte Square. The four of them crossed the street to the park and sat in a row on a bench. There was silence at first; finally the bigger guard with the moustache stood up and faced them.

"Where is it?" he asked, towering over Rory. "The money."

Rory had done his homework. He knew about a pub on Broughton Street that homosexuals were known to frequent. He went there late in the evening, hoping the place would be full and he would be able to sneak in unnoticed. He wasn't disappointed, as the bar was crowded and smoky. He had a pint, and asked a few of the men about the two guards, surprised at how easy it was for him to turn on the man-to-man charm; even more surprised at how openly they responded. They all knew Big Red and his friend, Graeme. Every Thursday before his overnight shift at the college he came in and met the smaller one at the corner table. *Before his shift?* Rory asked. *How much drink can he handle?* he said, faking admiration, ordering a round for the table. *Plenty,* he was told. *Everyone knows Red is Big about everything,* one of the men told him, winking.

Big Red was married, as he'd told them that night at Summerhall. And he had four children. This will be easy, Rory thought to himself.

"So," he asked the two men, noticing that the smaller one was dressed well for the meeting in a crisp white shirt and polished shoes. "What is it that keeps the two of you occupied down on Broughton Street?"

"I'll kill you," said Big Red, swinging at Rory. "I'll kill you with my own hands."

"And how are the little ones?" Rory asked, taunting the man.

"I'd watch what you're saying there," the smaller one said, looking over at Skye. "We have evidence about her carrying on."

"Look, Graeme," said Rory. "Now that the dirt is on the table, why don't we all just walk away and call this whole thing even. I wouldn't want to have to go to your boss. I wouldn't want to have to tell his wife."

Graeme looked at Big Red and the look sent shivers down Skye's spine. It was tender. No, it was tragic and desperate. "Please?" he asked.

●

When they didn't return to Summerhall, Skye assumed that the night watchmen found the money elsewhere. She was relieved, although slightly guilty for not helping out where she could have. It was Rory who told her the news. "The big one hanged himself," he said. "I saw the smaller one sitting alone on that very bench where we'd left them. He told me that the wife had read the note that he'd left her when he thought they'd be off to America on a boat. She went to Big Red's boss, and she also went to everyone in his family."

"How sad," Skye said.

"How selfish. What about his kids? He took the coward's way out."

"I imagine it's more complicated than that," Skye said. "It's easy to call someone a coward when it's not you trying to live in his skin."

●

The waves of nausea were undeniable and the morning sickness confirmed what her missing period had suggested. Skye met Rory in a tea shop on King George IV Bridge. It seemed like an impossible conversation, but she had to have it. She knew where the chloroform was kept at the college and where there were appropriate instruments and a table.

"And you're coming," she'd told Rory. "You're holding my hand until the deed is done."

Rory nodded and kissed Skye on the forehead. The shop was filling up so he lowered his voice.

"Of course I'll hold your hand," he whispered. "But are you sure you want to do this?"

"I'm certain...about what I don't want," she said.

The doctor she saw said he could help. He said he understood that she had a problem *down there*, said he could fix it for the right money under the table.

"Things will be different in Canada. You can still do your work with animals," Rory said. "We could bring in some help for the baby."

"There'll be no help," Skye told him. "I don't want a family now and I'm not saying goodbye to Mum and Dad with this secret in my belly."

"Whatever you want," he said, but Skye knew he didn't mean it. She could tell by his watery eyes and by the way his whole body shook with grief when he handed her the money for the doctor's *off the table in ten minutes* treatment.

•

It didn't take ten minutes, it took much longer. She came to once and could hear him tell Rory to keep the gauze over her nose and mouth. The chloroform made her sick for days and she didn't think the bleeding would ever stop. She was angrier than she thought she'd be at Rory; but mostly she was angry at herself, and the bastard who charged her extra for taking out twins.

•

Her mother didn't open her mouth, not a single word was ever spoken about the issue. She brought Skye special teas and made her hearty soups. Once, she even rubbed between her shoulders as she was being sick. But this all happened after she'd dragged Skye from a deep sleep filled with fitful dreams of foetuses and the animals that must have come in and out of the dissecting room at Summerhall. There was the troubled spirit of a dog with a broken leg, and a ghostly lamb with a suggestive smile. There were pigs with elephant ears, and a monkey with two heads and a rat's tail. There were two human foetuses in a pool of blood on the floor by the bed. Skye was grateful that something had woken her, but she wished she could go back to the relative safety of her nightmare when she saw the clump of muddied, blood-stained underclothing, held out in her mother's shaking hand.

# KINCARDINE, 1981

From her side of the bed, Skye saw out the window to the overhang of the attic where the squirrel had dug in. It was only a few feet away, she could almost touch the chicken wire that Rory had nailed across the entrance hole between the eavestrough and the roof. He'd hung out the window, and from inside the bedroom she held on to his belt. He was determined to be useful, though he was so ill that his legs were unsteady and his pants hung off him. She had no idea what she would do if he started to fall.

At first there was nothing to see, only darkness and stars above the house. Most nights she could hear the squirrel above them as she watched the subtle rise and fall of Rory's chest while he slept — still breathing, although hardly noticeable. Then one night, wakened by a bright, full moon and a weighted silence, Skye looked out through the dark and was certain she saw something above the chicken wire. She closed her eyes, placed one hand on her husband's chest and gripped the edge of the mattress with the other. When she looked again, she saw the sparkling of the squirrel's shiny eyes. It did not move, but she was sure those black eyes were pleading. She'd told Rory to make sure the squirrel was out before sealing the hole; clearly the squirrel had never left the attic. There was a gasp and then the slow rattle from Rory's side of the bed; she pressed her hand gently against his chest and turned to face him. She couldn't see any sign of breathing. *Damn you*, she whispered, when she pressed again and couldn't find a pulse. *Curse you.* She looked up through the dark and wept.

•

Skye stepped out of the shower and stood on the balls of her feet. She reached up to the ceiling, then bent to touch her toes. The days and weeks after Rory's death were tough. She'd always considered herself independent, a loner who just happened to have a husband. But now she missed him terribly and wondered how she would get by. Each day, in an effort to keep moving, she performed the same exercise ritual — reach for the stars, roll to the earth: *repeat as necessary*, she told herself.

At night she heard scratching in the attic. It was steady and frantic, and she couldn't sleep. She turned on her side and put the pillow over her ears, but her conscience got to her and she went down to the kitchen and spoke into the wall where they'd placed the chicken wire. *I'll call a contractor tomorrow*, she whispered, *just go to sleep tonight*. But she never made the call. And when night time came and she could hear scratching, the frantic attempt to break out; she would get out of bed and whisper again: *go to sleep. Just go for tonight.*

•

She was the expert on animals and it was Rory's job to do the repairs around the house. He was the handyman and builder. Skye had mentioned the squirrel in the attic; she'd even shown him how it probably got in through a small hole between the eavestrough and the roof. At first, her complaint fell on deaf ears; Rory was preoccupied with something more urgent. It started with blood in his urine, then quickly spread to his kidney and liver; the cancer that took him was diagnosed in April; he was dead by November. It seemed impossible to Skye; up until that point in his life, her husband was the picture of health. A decent man with fire in his bones; busy as a Scottish wood ant, strong as a plough horse.

The first time the squirrel got into the house it wreaked havoc in the kitchen. They learned later that it came down from the attic through a gap in the drywall behind the stove, throwing papers on the floor, eating the avocado and tomatoes they'd left on the table, urinating and defecating throughout the house. At first they thought someone had broken in, the way everything was thrown about. Then they saw tiny prints on the counters and around the kitchen sink. It was easy to plug up the hole with chicken wire. The squirrel would learn that she couldn't gain access to food and she'd go away. But she didn't go away; she was caged in. Skye heard her at night between the wall slats trying to get out. She probably had a nest up there, or in the high branches of a nearby tree; soon there'd be an entire family of scratchy little feet above her head keeping her awake.

•

The moment of self-awareness was shocking. The fact that she could leave a living creature trapped in her attic and not go to its rescue was shocking to Skye. She had watched it claw at the wire mesh, she had watched it pant with exhaustion and thirst. She was trained to save animals, but she didn't. She witnessed the squirrel looking down on her before it disappeared into the dark; listened to it scratch at the attic walls night after night.

•

Her life wasn't wasted, but sometimes she felt otherwise. Skye did her best by Rory and Duncan — but Moira, the people in town talked about how pretty she was, *such a smart little girl,* they would say. *How proud you must be of your first-born.*

•

A few days after Rory died, Skye went down to the basement and uncovered the large trunk that he'd carried with him overseas. Skye always considered it sacred male territory — the place where he kept his war helmet, boots, and military fatigues. She knew that his war medals were in there, and she was aware that he had several pictures of Moira in the trunk as well. But she had to sit on the cold cement floor when she discovered the blue box, the one that he had presented to her wrapped in a white hankie that he'd tied together with a band of red silk from his cap. He kept them all these years, those terrible caskets — the miniscule evidence of what she had done. How terribly misguided of him. What ever could have possessed him to do such a thing?

*It's for your suffering*, he'd said. *To help you remember.*

As if she could forget. All the years of trying, and nothing worked. The College was meant to be Skye's safe haven, the place where she was to thrive and be happy. But the sexual overtones among her classmates were always there. She'd felt uneasy about what was expected of her by men and, until Rory came marching along, she'd managed to avoid the inevitable. Established by William Dick, Summerhall was called Dick Vet back then or, for the more brazen girls, *the Royal Dick*. From the beginning she should have known what would come of her there.

Moira's birth was a reminder — *You have a sister and a brother, Moira Rayburn, twin ghosts*, she said to herself the day her daughter was born.

One miniature casket with an *M* carved into it, and one with an *R* — each with the figure of an infant inside. Rory had gone to great lengths to console her. A young man with his heart in the right place — but his brain — what was he thinking? *How could you be so morbid?* she remembers asking him as the smile on his face turned down.

She could smell the chloroform for months after, and the pain and bleeding took weeks to stop. *Stupid girl*, she chastised herself. *Stupid, stupid girl.* She'd hoped that once they'd left her belly they would vanish, scatter to the ether like a pair of windblown clouds. Well, they didn't, and the annoying little caskets cherished and hidden by Rory all these years were a reminder. *But why?* Skye asked herself, holding one of the miniature caskets in her hand — a sorry deed, encased by her young lover's careful etching. *Why would he cling to such horrible grief?*

# KINCARDINE, 1987

Every Saturday night at sunset all summer long, the bagpipers made their way down Kincardine's main street; followed by Blinky, the town's lighthouse mascot, and then by the town's people. Skye held Duncan's hand as he jumped up and down.

"There's your friend from Scotland, Grandma Skye," he yelled. "There's Graeme!"

Graeme was old, but he had a steady stride. He led the bagpipe parade the way he always had since his arrival in Kincardine in 1945.

•

"Find him," Skye had said to Rory the day he told her about Big Red's suicide. "Find the little one, Graeme. He has to come with us."

"You're joking?" Rory said.

"No, I am not joking. It's partly our fault. We could have helped, but we didn't."

"He has no passage, where would he stay? Besides," Rory said. "He wants New York, not Kincardine."

"He wanted a new life with someone — that someone is dead now. That someone has killed himself, but that doesn't mean he should be deprived of a chance to start anew."

# KINCARDINE, 1990

It was a perfect morning with crisp winter light and a thin dusting of snow covering the old. Rocky ran ahead of Skye, weaving in and out of bushes, darting between rows of pine and spruce, chasing birds or a scent he'd discovered under a fallen tree or stone. Skye soon forgot about the rambunctious dog as her memory of the journey to Canada pulled her back.

They had taken a boat from Leith. It was filled mostly with soldiers and their young brides. The voyage would take several days and she didn't feel up to it. Rory seemed to understand, but there were only so many boats, and he was anxious to get home. The day before their departure, they had a small marriage ceremony in Holyrood Park with her girlfriend, Anne, and her husband, as witnesses. After vows were taken, she and Rory walked alone to Arthur's Seat where they'd had their first kiss just a few months earlier. Things had changed so irreversibly that she hardly knew who she was. Skye looked over the rolling hills and out to the sea. Nothing she had done up to that point in her life could have prepared her for this. She'd taken an oath to help alleviate suffering in animals — she wondered where an abortion fit into the scheme of things?

The boat was crowded, and she was grateful for the privacy of their small cabin. Rory sat next to her on the bunk and held the pot for her when she was sick. And when she put her head down on the pillow to try to sleep while the boat heaved and rocked, he held her close and told her stories about Canada. *Where we're going to live there's a forest right off the beach*, he told her. *In the winter you*

*can walk or snowshoe, and all year round there are trails along the lake
shore and through the forest.*

Skye was jolted out of her thoughts by a yelp. She knew it was
serious. Rocky came limping through the snow with his paw in the
air. There were dozens of quills embedded in his paws and face. In
all her years as a veterinarian, she'd never seen anything this bad. He
must have gotten very close to the porcupine. She pulled out what
she could from his paws, lips and cheeks. The dog wasn't the hunting
type; she was sure he would have been wagging his tail and barking.
She bent to pick him up, leaving droplets of blood in the snow as
they walked back through the forest to her truck on the side of the
road.

●

On the second day of the boat trip to Canada, Rory gave her a
present. He had been secretly carving something, she knew by the
shavings on the floor by the bed. He gave it to her wrapped in a
white hankie he'd tied together with a band of red silk that he'd
removed from his military cap.

"Rory," she'd said. "What's this?"

"It's for your suffering," he'd said. "And to help you remember."

She felt a wave of nausea and had to place her head on her
knees to stop from being sick again.

"I don't want to remember," she'd said.

Rory stood facing her. He knelt on one knee and kissed her
hand. The ring on her finger was plain and silver. There was no
stone in it yet, but Rory promised he would have a diamond put in
it when they got to Canada. He kissed her ring hand again.

"This will make you feel better," he said, nudging her to
unwrap her present.

He was anxious and childlike; she couldn't imagine the man
kneeling in front of her capable of killing another, even in war.
Then again, her perception of the world was changing fast. She
felt another wave of nausea, and put her head down on the small
package which she held in her hands.

After a few seconds she lifted her head and undid the ribbon. The handkerchief fell back like a soft white flower exposing the small blue box that he had been given his war medals in.

"You didn't," she said. "Not your medals?"

"Better," he said. "Something I made."

Skye lifted the lid and inside there were two wooden coffins about the size of matchstick boxes. She lifted one of the tiny caskets, light as a feather, and held it up to the light of the porthole. She slid off the lid with an M etched on it. What was he thinking? Rory had taken great care to carve out the figure of an infant inside. She didn't know what to say when he asked if she liked it. She picked up the second box with an R on it. The detail was extraordinary — miniscule wooden handles to lift the coffin, dovetailed sides, and a cross beneath each initial.

"R for Rory," he said, as she set the second coffin back in the blue box next to the other. "I would have liked to give my first-born son my name."

"What's the M?" she asked him, picking up the other box again.

"M, for Moira, like your mother," he said.

Skye's head started spinning and she couldn't wait for the pot. She was sick on the bed, and again on the floor.

"My mother?" she said, wiping her mouth. "How could you be so morbid?" she asked, handing him the blue box with the coffins.

•

On the third day, she began to feel better about the boat, and welcomed those moments when she'd be sitting on a bench on the upper deck looking across the water. Sunlight danced on the rolling waves, and there was a tiny quiver of hope in her stomach. She thought about how her girlfriend Anne had told her that Canada was a rough, beautiful country, a place where she could start new, with a clean slate. Rory sat with her, carving out a doll for one of the many children travelling on the boat. There hadn't been much time for anything, let alone an explanation of her relationship with her parents, but Skye felt she had better be honest with Rory.

"My mother had three priorities in life," she'd told him. "She called them the three M's."

Rory stopped carving and looked up at her. "Three M's?"

"Money, manners and marriage," she said. "My mother said that everything in life comes down to these three things."

"Everything?" Rory asked.

"Everything," Skye said, twisting the ring on her finger.

Rory went back to his carving, cutting away the details of arms and legs, etching miniature buttons into the doll's jacket.

"And what about money, manners and marriage?" he said, setting the doll and the knife down on the bench between them.

Skye had never tried to articulate this before, but she felt that she should try.

"Well," she said. "My mother said that a girl had to have money to get by in the world. She said never marry down. She said that they were prepared to pay for my education, but I would need to marry well to carry myself properly in the world."

"That's enough," Rory said. "I take it that's the real reason they didn't come to the wedding — you didn't marry *up* enough?"

Skye felt ashamed to say yes, but she nodded her head. The day they were married, she'd told Rory that her parents had come down with a sudden virus.

She had tried to convince them that she would do well as a veterinarian in Canada, and that Rory too would step up to his calling as a craftsman. *That snowbound country has no society*, her mother said. *You'll end up abandoned and living in some small backward town with a dozen children pulling at your skirts.*

Skye tried to explain. She took her father's hand, but he pulled away and marched out of the sitting room.

*He fought in the war, Father*, Skye said to his back as he was leaving. *The man has courage and dignity.*

*Tales of courage are used by those boys to get you where they want*, her mother interjected. *And don't tell me about dignity; your father's company practically gives away those serge pants they wear to parade down the streets of Edinburgh...*

Vannan Wool and Manufacturing had done well with the war. It was undeniable to Skye that her father had become wealthy as a result of the demand for sturdy uniforms from an established clothing maker.

*…the shipload of girls with babies in their bellies that leave the Gourock docks every week is proof enough for me,* her mother went on.

Skye couldn't look at her, so her mother took her face in her hands and turned her around. There was hardly a hair's distance between her mother's eyes and hers. *You are not in the family way?* her mother had asked. Skye was relieved that she was able to say at that point that she wasn't. But her mother saw right through her. *If I ever find out otherwise…*she said…*you will be denied your inheritance.*

•

Skye set Rocky down on the back seat of the truck. He continued to whimper but didn't complain when she removed a quill from above his eye. She needed to get him home where she had proper instruments and something to sedate him. She should have known he would find a porcupine. He was due for trouble — there had already been two skunks earlier in the month and he'd nearly caused someone to drive off Inverness when he ran out in the road chasing a squirrel.

# KINCARDINE, 1999

The day they'd worked on the Layton campaign, Duncan had a difficult time with one of the callers and Siobhan knew exactly what to say. She was a rough, scrappy girl, but Skye was learning to respect that she had a watchful eye for Duncan.

"Where did you say that you live, Siobhan?" she asked.

"I didn't," she said, looking at Skye from the corner of her eye. "But I live at the Royal Apartments. With my mother."

"And how old did you say you were?"

"I didn't say how old I was, Skye," she answered, sounding distinctly more defensive. "But if you're asking," she added, "I'm two years younger than Duncan and Squirrely Shirley *is* my mother."

And as Skye absorbed the information, Siobhan added a final damning statement: "I'm sure you've seen her rolling in and out of the Bruce Tavern over the years."

"Do you look like her or your father?" Skye asked, pushing a little further.

But the telephone rang, and as Siobhan answered, Duncan gave Skye his best *don't go there* look.

As the afternoon went on, Skye watched Duncan and Siobhan working together and her head filled with memories of the day she walked in on Magnus with Shirley Kellins, half naked on the bedroom floor at the Royal Apartments. Skye had been disgusted — the beer bottles and leftover Chinese, the piles of dirty clothes scattered around the room.

*Skye Rayburn?* Shirley Kellins had asked. *Is that you?*

But she hadn't answered. She was furious and vowed to strangle the woman if she saw her again.

Duncan had enough shame to carry. A runaway father *and* the town tramp's daughter as a sister — that would simply be too much burden for one young man to shoulder.

# KINCARDINE, 2001

Skye told him that the first word he learned to say was *bird*. She said that the blue jays and crows were fighting in a tree in the back yard and he pointed to them and said *Bir Bir*.

"What was the second word I spoke?" Duncan asked.

Skye paused for a long time. She appeared to be thinking, but she also looked afraid.

"I can't remember," she said, gathering her paper and pencils off the table.

"You!" Duncan said. "You're like an elephant, you never forget anything."

"Well, I'm not 100% sure what word you spoke next, perhaps it was *car* or *apple*?"

Duncan had the feeling that Skye wasn't telling him the truth. Trust your intuition, she'd always told him, so he asked her again. "Are you sure?"

They had been drawing together at the kitchen table, and the day was perfect. Duncan was proud of what he'd been learning at Western, and he was happy to be home for March break, showing Skye a new drawing technique. *Like this, Grandma Skye*, he'd explained, showing her how to relax her hand. *Allow the pencil to flow across the page to make wings or waves. Like this*, he said, drawing an oval for the shell of a person's face, and then mapping out spaces for his subject's eyes, mouth and nose.

"It was *ma ma*," Skye finally confessed. "You asked for your mother a few months after she died."

"What's the big deal about that?" Duncan said. "I imagine those are the first words out of most kids' mouths."

"There's more" said Skye, standing and turning to leave the kitchen, "that I won't get into."

"Okay, now you have to tell. You can't just drop a bomb like that and think I'm not going to ask you for more."

Skye sighed and sat back down at the table.

"You saw her," she said. "We were in the upstairs room, and you pointed to your mother in a chair by your bed."

Duncan was ecstatic that Skye had finally spoken about this. He stood up and walked over to the end of the table where she was sitting: "Thank you thank you thank you," he said, kissing her on the cheek, "for finally saying something."

"You were always like that," Skye said. "Seeing things that others couldn't. Talking to your imaginary friends."

"They weren't imaginary," he said. "At times I thought I was going crazy. I did see Grandpa Rory after he died. I even saw the squirrel that died in the attic."

It was Skye's turn to be shocked.

"What?"

"The squirrel," he said. "You know how you've always talked about patching the hole in the wall behind the stove after you found that dead squirrel there."

"Yes. Yes," Skye said. "But you were just a toddler."

"It landed on my bed," Duncan told her. "I woke up because I could feel it."

"Did it harm you? Were you frightened? Why didn't you tell me!"

"Slow down, Grandma Skye. I guess because I was just a kid, the whole thing seemed natural and fun."

"What do you mean, the whole thing?"

"Well, the squirrel didn't talk, but I understood her. She wanted me to go to my bedroom window."

"Yes," said Skye, her hand shaking as she attempted to sip her tea.

"The squirrel had babies. A nest of them in the tree next to the house and she wanted me to save them."

"My goodness," Skye said. "That's impossible."

"She asked me to go downstairs and open the door. She told me to let the cat in the house. And I did."

"All by yourself?" said Skye.

"All by myself," said Duncan. "I let the cat in the house and the squirrel went away."

# PART VIII

## DOG

| Species | Canis lupus familiaris |
|---|---|
| Phylum | Chordata |
| Order | Carnivora |
| Family | Canidae |
| Description | The domestic dog ranges in height from a few inches to a few feet in length; varying colours and a wide range of coats; they have two ears, a tail, and four legs. |
| Attributes | Aside from being man's best friend — dogs hunt, herd, and assist handicapped individuals. |

Life Lesson for Duncan

Love. Loyalty. Trust.

# KINCARDINE, 1995

Glucosamine and chondroitin no longer helped with the arthritis in his hind legs. His sight was going, and he almost never made it outside to do his business. As Skye bent down to wipe the floor, she looked over at Rocky, sleeping on his tattered straw basket in the hallway. From the first day that she brought him home, he'd always slept there — halfway between her bedroom and Duncan's. She'd removed porcupine quills from his paws; she'd scrubbed skunk stink from his coat. She'd fed and walked him, and scratched behind his ears — and each and every gesture of affection was returned twentyfold.

Over the years, Rocky listened as she talked from her heart about Scotland — her mother's attempts to rope her in; and how her father managed to stand at peace in the middle. He sat quietly as she fretted and talked about that awful puppy mill, or the farmer being unfaithful to his long-suffering wife. He listened as she worried out loud about Moira and Duncan, and he'd helped her decide what to do about Siobhan. He didn't say a word, of course, but Skye knew that he understood by the way he thumped his heavy tail against the hardwood floor.

*I can't tell Duncan*, she told Rocky. *What good would it do? Besides,* she reasoned, *it's the mother's job to tell the daughter who the father is. Perhaps it isn't even Magnus? After all, the whole town is aware of Shirley Kellin's reputation.* But Skye knew that she was only fooling herself. Siobhan had her father's bone structure and his mischievous smile. And those blue-green eyes, they were exact duplicates — even the gold ring that circled the irises were like his.

No more chasing the squirrel or barking at the feral cat in the yard, Rocky could no longer do the things that he loved. She fed him a bowl of his favourite food — diced chicken livers, slightly steamed. And when he finished what he could, she took away the bowl and scratched his neck. She sat beside him on the floor and gently massaged his hind legs. She lifted his head onto her lap and whispered *thank you* in his ear, inhaled his musty smell one last time. *Thank you, dear friend*, she whispered. She took off his collar and set it next to her. It was snowing, and she could feel the cold from under the floorboards. She placed his grey blanket over him and used the gold silk from her mother as a tourniquet on his back leg where she knew there would be little sensation and he would be least likely to feel the needle. She injected the pentobarbital into his hip and waited. She counted backwards from ten and when she was certain he was gone, she placed her hand over his eyes and closed them. She stayed with him a long time. Her grey hair hanging down and her shoulders bent forward, she sat stroking his black coat over and over.

When she opened her eyes, the hallway was dark and Rocky was gone; so was the blanket, collar, his bowl, the gold silk cloth, and the needle she had used for the injection. Perhaps she had dreamt the whole thing and Rocky was still with her, wandering down the hallway to Duncan's room? Skye pressed her back against the wall and tried to stand but didn't have the strength to get off the floor. Inch by inch, she slid along the hallway to the top of the stairs.

"Rocky," she shouted. "Here, boy." But there was no answer as she swung her legs onto the top stair.

"Skye," she heard Duncan call. "Stay put, I'm coming."

When Duncan came running up the stairs, his face was pink from the cold and she could see snow on his boots and mud on his trousers.

"I put him in the backyard," he said, trying to catch his breath, "under the tree next to Thistle."

Duncan helped her down the stairs, one at a time, to the bottom.

"The ground is almost frozen solid," he said, still breathing hard.

Skye steadied herself on the handrail and looked at her grandson. "You're a godsend," she said.

He brought Skye's walker to where she stood at the bottom of the stairs and together they moved slowly to the back door. As they looked across the yard and onto the square of mud that Duncan had dug in the snow next to where they had buried Thistle, Skye's eyes began to well up.

*Twin graves*, Skye thought.

The two of them turned from the yard and walked down the hallway toward the light of the kitchen. And as she stepped into the room, Skye saw Rocky's empty bowl next to his collar on the table. The syringe was not there and she was grateful not to have to look at it again. He is free now, Skye thought, looking down at the collar. He's racing through the forest after sparrows and skunks — darting and diving, chasing his shadow across the snow, pausing every now and then to look back for her, not so far behind, bent into the path that winds up to the hill.

# KINCARDINE, 2011

From the beginning, Skye had planned on keeping *Life Lessons* light-hearted and playful. It was written with Duncan in mind and never intended to be her journal, but the minute Duncan boarded the plane for Edinburgh, she began writing things that took her by surprise.

*Some people shouldn't own animals*, she began, *and some people shouldn't have children.* All these years later, she was suddenly compelled to write about the puppies in that barn and the children in that filthy house. *Life isn't what I thought it would be*, she continued; *it hasn't been for a long time. I've told you some things about all those dogs stacked in cages in the barn. I've told you about the hoarding and the parents who didn't see anything wrong with how they lived. I gave you some of the horrible details of the neglect but I've never told you how it became impossible after that experience for me to see human beings the same way. I was filled with concern for animals and fear for the children. I felt helpless, and remained that way for a long time, until finally, out of the blue one day I started to understand your father. Perhaps he knew he couldn't raise you properly? Perhaps his desertion was an act of compassion for you?*

*Grandfather Rory and I carved our initials into the wall at Summerhall. I was nervous and hopeful in the same breath. We used a grouse foot kilt pin that my mother gave me for my nineteenth birthday; a meaningless object to most people, but everything to us. We brought it out on our anniversary day each year. We brought it out when we bought this house and when Moira was born. I brought it out when you were a child and came to live with me. When Rory died I wore it on my scarf. And now, I have given it to your father, and he will be bringing it back to you. Don't be surprised if he knocks on the door. Don't push him away. Take what he gives you for what it is, a worthless brooch; but look beyond the dirt of the man who puts it in your hand. There's a light about you, Sweet Boy, Duncan, don't let anyone take it. But...* she starts, needing to set her pen down and reach deep into her thoughts ... *share that light; open your heart, especially when it's your father standing in front of you.*

•

As Cathy gets close to the house on Princes Street, she thinks back to the day when she had first brought her daughter to meet Skye. Little Moira had sat at the end of the table eating ice cream like a grown-up and Cathy was proud of her.

"She's adorable. You must be a good mother," Skye had told her, and Cathy knew the visit would be perfect.

"I brought you something," she told Skye, reaching into her bag and pulling out the present. Cathy could hardly wait to give Skye her gift.

"Do you remember the song I played at Moira's funeral?" she asked.

"Yes," said Skye, her hands shaking as she unwrapped the present. "I had switched my wedding ring onto the wrong finger so that I would remember to look up the lyrics, but I never did. The ring stayed on that finger for a week, and I still couldn't remember what I was reminding myself of."

"Switched your wedding ring?"

"An old habit," Skye said. "My way of trying to remember things; it's a trick that doesn't always work."

Skye held in her hand a book with a beautiful, brown leather cover. She took her time holding it, feeling the weight of it before turning to the first page. Inside, in large bold letters: *BACK IN BLACK* written across the page; beneath the title, a rough drawing of what looked like an animal's eye.

"Little Moira did all of the pictures," Cathy told her, hardly able to contain her excitement. "That's a cat's eye. Turn the next page!" she said. "It's all the words to the song done with pictures."

*Looking at the Skye 'cause it's getting me high* is written across the top of the page, and beneath it, a stick drawing of a very tall woman holding a cat with its paw wrapped in a bandage.

"That's you," little Moira said. She had come to stand by Skye and was leaning against her side as she turned the pages.

"It is indeed," Skye said, kissing the child on the forehead.

Skye put the book down and began to sob — deep, deep, tears.

"I've never seen anything so beautiful," she said, hugging Moira while looking over at her mother.

"Get it?" said Cathy. "…Sky with an e on the end, instead of the regular sky."

"Oh, I get it," Skye told Cathy, hugging Moira again.

•

Cathy rings the doorbell and waits a few minutes before letting herself in with the key that Duncan had given her before leaving for his trip. It was good to be out of the heat and standing inside the old, cool house. She hears voices in the kitchen and feels relieved. "Skye?" she calls out. "It's Cathy."

She thinks about what Duncan told her: *I've been calling her and calling her, she's not picking up the phone, something's wrong.* She knows that Duncan worries too much about Skye, but she also knows that Skye is old, and probably shouldn't have been left alone all this time.

The day after Duncan left for Scotland, Cathy left her daughter with a sitter and brought Skye a cake. She'd worked hard on it, wanting to impress Skye with her baking.

"It's a Queen Elizabeth cake," she told Skye, as she set it down at the kitchen table. "It has pecans, dates and coconut."

Skye had a large piece and praised Cathy for her baking and for being so considerate.

"I never did learn to do much in the kitchen," she said. "But ask me how to remove a porcupine's quill from the paw of a dog and I'm right on it."

They sat quietly for a while and both had a second piece of cake. When Cathy left, Skye seemed fine. No sign of the heart problems Duncan had told her about; no sign of confusion or dementia. Sure, she couldn't find her reading glasses, but who hasn't misplaced their glasses before? Yes, she was awkward on her walker, but pretty darn good for someone her age!

•

Cathy is overcome with dread. It's the same gold and green-trimmed house where she and Moira would sit on the porch as young girls; the same house where everyone met for sandwiches after Moira's funeral, except her. The same house where she eventually brought her own Moira to meet the woman she once hated; only it seems darker, and somehow quieter, even from the outside.

•

"She knows everything about animals," Cathy would tell her daughter, as she played with her plastic pony in the sandbox behind their apartment. "She raised her grandson on her own while she worked like a dog."

"Woof woof," her daughter barked.

"I don't mean a real dog, Moira. It's just an expression grown-ups use."

•

But as much as Cathy praised her virtues, there was something about Skye that was difficult to accept. Skye was a hard worker, and smart. She could outwit anyone Cathy knew. She either loved or hated you, there was no in between, and Cathy wasn't one hundred percent sure that Skye had loved her own daughter. Once, when they were about fourteen, she and Moira had stayed out past the ten o'clock curfew. Moira had begged her to walk her home and help with the excuse.

Moira told Skye that Cathy sprained her ankle and it took hours to walk home. *Right Cath, show her your foot.*

They had rubbed the foot to make it red, and Cathy had limped up to the door. Skye felt the foot for swelling and heat, told Cathy to put ice on it when she got home. She offered Cathy a ride, but she turned down the offer. *Run off then,* Skye told her. *I need to have a few words with Moira,* and slammed the door. Cathy didn't leave though. She sat on the porch in the wicker chair by the window. *Do you think I'm a fool?* Skye yelled at Moira. *You think I can't judge whether an ankle is sprained? You think I don't know a liar when I'm looking at one?*

●

It doesn't take long for Cathy to realize the voices she is hearing are voices from the kitchen radio. The news about Jack Layton was on every radio in town, and there it was again: *…funeral services to be held at Toronto's Roy Thomson Hall this Saturday.* She smells smoke, and as she gets closer, she sees Skye curled in a ball on the floor.

●

Skye turned on the radio when she first went into the kitchen. She listened to the CBC every morning of her adult life. She was cold, but still couldn't lift herself off the floor. *Jack Layton is dead,* the announcer said. *Cancer.* The pain in her chest had stopped and she could breathe easier; maybe she should just stay put. *Jack Layton is dead, how sad,* she whispered. She placed her head on the cool linoleum and wondered about Duncan; so far away, his first trip overseas. She hadn't noticed the smoke had become worse until she rolled onto her back. Adrenaline? Fear? A last-ditch effort to live long enough to see Duncan safely home? Whatever the reason, she found the strength to sit up. *Duncan Johnson,* she said out loud. She rolled onto her side, and then faced down. She pushed herself up and placed her hands on the side of the chair that had toppled along with her. *There's plenty I have to tell you yet!,* she said, pulling herself up off the floor.

Skye eased her way through the smoke over to the stove where the pot was burning. The telephone had woken her, ringing over and over: *Duncan*. She began coughing and couldn't catch her breath. She grabbed the handle and pain shot through her hand, and the pot fell to the floor. And at that very instant she thought back to the day when she went to the bank for the money. *A certified cheque won't work,* she told the cashier. *I need five thousand dollars in cash.* The tightening in her chest worsened and the room began to spin as she fell to floor.

•

When Skye opened her eyes, she heard voices; it took a few seconds to realize it was the radio. *Jack Layton, dead at sixty-one,* the announcer said. *His funeral will be held at Roy Thomson Hall, August 31.* The smoke in the kitchen had cleared but the pain in her was still there.

She rememberd orange T-shirts, orange balloons and name tags — Siobhan and Duncan campaigning from the house. "It's the only party that makes sense," said Siobhan, and for the first time ever, the three of them found common ground.

"I agree," Skye told her. Duncan smiled and kissed his grandmother on the cheek.

"Thanks for letting us do this here," he said. "Siobhan's place at the Royal is pretty small."

They folded newsletters and called everyone in the phone book. Skye was happy to be with them. She had worried a lot about Duncan over the years. He was trusting of people; to the point, at times, of being naïve. Siobhan wasn't really bad, she'd figured out; and, most importantly, she'd go to bat for Duncan no matter what.

They had a rule, if someone being canvassed hung up the telephone on one of them, all three would have a moment of silence and a cookie out of respect. After the fifth hang-up and cookie, Siobhan said, "This isn't going to work. We'll never get anything done with all this downtime and cookie munching."

Skye laughed and spat out her cookie; and so did Duncan.

"We have to get over feeling bad about hang-ups," he said, and the three of them went back to work on the phones.

But as they worked, Skye watched Siobhan.

Another sharp pain in her side, Skye closed her eyes. She thought about Duncan in Edinburgh. She wandered the cobblestone, searched the misty streets and lush hills: *Duncan*.

# EDINBURGH, 2011

The spirit of a hundred thousand dead animals is an elephant — no, she's a dog and a horse and a snake; red as a fox; flying like a sparrow, flicking droplets of rain off her wings. Duncan feels her in gusts of cool rain as he walks down the street. He calls Skye on his cellphone — knowing why she doesn't answer, refusing to believe what he sees in the clouds hanging over Broughton Street.

At the Blue Moon, he places his backpack with sketchbook and cellphone at the same table where he sat the day he met Paul. So much has happened since that day, he's happy to be in an environment that feels familiar. Siobhan will be late; they agreed on an hour and a half, but she will take two. He orders a coffee from the waiter and takes out his pencils and sketchbook, but can't concentrate on drawing. He doodles as the rain splashes against the window — even *it* sounds like staccato fragments of Skye's weakened voice. He tries to put her out of his mind, but can't help himself — he listens for a message in the strong gusts of wind. He stands and paces. Back at the table he picks up his cellphone and dials Kincardine. This time, after four rings someone finally answers.

"Who's this?" he blurts into the phone.

"Who's this?" a female voice on the other end asks.

"It's Duncan," he says. "Is Skye all right?"

"Skye?" the woman says. "Sorry, you have the wrong number."

Duncan dials the number carefully, one more time, and listens to it ring eight times before hanging up.

He walks downstairs and goes into the washroom and sits. There's a knock on the door, and Siobhan's tentative voice.

"Duncan, is that you?"

He opens the door and she's standing there, soaking wet, out of breath and smelling of cigarettes.

"I ran all the way," she says, panting. "I didn't have a single pound left for bus fare. I just smoked my second-last cigarette."

"How did you know it was me in here?" he says.

"Because every time I can't find you in Scotland, you're in some washroom."

"Really?"

"No, you fool, your art stuff is on the table in the window and there are only so many places to go in this place. You look awful."

"Thanks," he says. "Just what I needed — kind words from a friend to lift my spirits."

He buys her a coffee and sandwich, and once they're back at the table he folds his arms and looks out the window.

"Does it *ever* stop raining here?" he says.

"Will the world *ever* come to its senses and allow smoking in coffee shops again?"

"Skye's dead," Duncan blurts out.

"What?"

"I said: Skye is dead."

"How do you know that? Did someone call?"

"No. But I've been calling her on my cell for two days and there's no answer. Besides," he says, "I just know."

"I think you're stressed," she says. "Could you be making this up so you have to go home early? Did you call Cathy — wasn't she looking in on her?"

After Moira's funeral, Cathy disappeared for a long time. Then, one day when Skye had almost forgotten about her, she showed up at the front door with a young child.

"This is my daughter," she told Skye. "I named her Moira."

Cathy said having a kid of her own changed things for her. She said that she understood better now. She said she was sorry for being rude to her at the funeral. Sometimes, when Cathy worked the night shift or weekends, she would leave little Moira with Skye.

And when she split up with her husband, she and Moira had stayed with them for two months.

"Yes, I called Cathy," Duncan said. "She said that she hadn't been to see Skye for a few days, but promised to go by tonight."

"Well, there you go," Siobhan said. "Cathy will check things out and everything will be fine. I think you're just making up an excuse to run away from a great shot at romance."

"How can you say that?"

"Because I know you. You're scared shitless of leaving that house on Princes, and you told me on the phone that Paul wants you to move here."

"Don't get me started on him," Duncan said. "He's called my cellphone three times in the last hour."

"He wants to be with you," said Siobhan. "There's nothing wrong with that."

●

There's a power outage and they have to leave the Blue Moon. As Duncan and Siobhan walk along Broughton Street they bump into Paul.

"I was on my way to your hotel," Paul says. "I've been calling your cellphone."

Siobhan doesn't say anything, but she smiles and steps back.

"I don't like the way our last conversation ended," he says to Duncan.

Duncan feels awkward. Paul is shivering, and looks sad. The rain is getting worse and the wind picks up. "Siobhan and I were just heading back to her hotel," he says. "Sorry …."

"But we need to talk," Paul says, handing him a bouquet of flowers and a small, wet package. "Open it."

"Not now," says Duncan, handing back the package and the flowers.

The street lights begin to flicker and Paul hands Duncan the flowers again. "Just a few minutes. Please?"

"The power is on again," Duncan says to Siobhan. "Can you wait for us at the Blue Moon?"

## BOA CONSTRICTOR

| | |
|---|---|
| Species | Boa constrictor |
| Phylum | Chordata |
| Order | Squamata |
| Family | Boidae |
| Description | Fawn or grey with reddish-brown "saddles," it's a heavy body snake; the female being larger in both length and girth than males. |
| Attributes | Nocturnal and solitary |

Life Lesson for Duncan
Stay alert — you never know when the ambush will come.

# TORONTO, 2008

Magnus needs enough money for the bus. He'll get cleaned up at the shelter, then walk to the bus station on Bay. He knows he can do it — fifty-seven cents more. You learn to smile and say God Bless because you're thankful when someone puts money in your Frisbee, and you mean it. You learn to smile and say God Bless because you want them to feel guilty for not giving you any money, and you hope they'll dig into their coat pockets and come back. You learn never to touch them, because they're afraid of germs. You learn not to look in their eyes, especially teenage boys, and to slowly pull in the Frisbee before they try to steal it. And you still don't look when one of them kicks you in the ribs and says, *get a job, loser*, and his two buddies laugh as they walk away, one of them bending to kiss Shania Twain's star on the Walk of Fame before running to catch up with the others.

•

Magnus makes the fifty-seven cents he needs for the bus, and two dollars more. But he doesn't make it past the liquor store. Just a small bottle, he tells himself, a mickey for the bus ride north. He shoves it into his inside coat pocket and walks down the street toward the men's shelter where he can have a shower. At the Shoppers Drug Mart, he catches his reflection in the window. He can hardly stand to look at his filthy, bearded face. He hangs his head and remembers Skye: *There's still time to be a father*, she said. He lifts his head and makes a decision to shave off the beard. He stands outside the door begging until he has enough change for blades and soap. *There's time,* he tries to convince himself. *Time for what?* he wonders, looking at the disgusting image of himself in the window. He curses and kicks the wall, sits on the sidewalk and reaches into his coat for the mickey; and when he stabs his finger on the stupid old brooch that Skye had given him to pass on to Duncan, he shouts as loud as he can: *Fuck you, Skye Rayburn.*

# TORONTO, 2008

**W**hen Black Hood Guy walked over to the outreach van with a dripping wet sleeping bag in one hand and the blue bag Magnus had told her about in the other, Jo knew she'd struck gold.

"You know that's not yours," she said, looking at the bag. Jo had long since learned that the only approach with street guys is the direct approach.

"Bullshit," he said.

"Bullshit to you too," she said, laughing. "Come on."

Jo didn't really expect the money to still be in the bag.

"Come on," she asked again, reaching out one hand for the bag and the other to give him his injection kit. "Come on."

There wasn't a hope in hell, she thought, until she heard the bleep of the cop car as it pulled into the empty parking lot at the back of Gerrard Square.

"I'll stall them," Jo told Black Hood Guy. "Leave the bag and I'll stall the cops."

Jo had street cred. Homeless people knew she was good for her word. As Black Hood Guy jumped over the fence to the train track, Jo walked through the rain to the police car.

"It's all good," she told the male officer who looked over at the bag on the pavement. "He was just dropping that off for his buddy."

The police were good for their word too. She'd asked them to keep watch for Black Hood Guy. She explained that every Sunday morning before the mall opens she makes a regular stop in the parking lot close to the tracks. *He just needs a little extra help right now,* she'd lied to the police after Magnus told her what happened.

"What about him?" the female officer asked, nodding to the fence as the GO train sped by spraying the fence with rain. "Should we track him down?"

"Don't think so," Jo said. "It's all good. He's off to dry out."

"You should do the same," the officer told her. "Get yourself out of the rain."

"I'll do that," she said, but her goal became more complicated once she discovered, among the photographs and a crack pipe, bundles of twenties, fives, fifties and tens.

*I'll keep it in trust for Magnus. Monday morning it goes to the Public Guardian and Trustee.*

## EDINBURGH, 2011

"I know I probably used the *L* word a little too early," Paul says, once Siobhan is out of earshot. "But I meant it."

"*A little too early* — are you kidding," Duncan says. "Nobody says *I love you* after less than a week."

"It happens when it happens, Duncan. Maybe can we start over and I can move at a slower pace?"

Paul hands him the package again and Duncan pulls a T-shirt out of the bag. The colours of the Scottish flag, the writing across the chest reads: INSIDE, I'M THE LIFE OF THE PARTY.

"I get you," Paul says. "And love who you are."

But before Duncan can say anything back, his cellphone rings. "Holy shit," he tells Paul, "hang on, it's Cathy."

•

The night of the kiss in Chalmer's Square they went back to Paul's apartment. Being in a different country with a really good-looking guy was both exciting and terrifying for Duncan. The neighbourhood looked exactly like those he'd seen in movies about Scotland — quiet, hilly streets with rows of quaint-looking townhouses squatting in darkness and drizzle. Duncan inhaled deeply and looked at Paul, so full of fire.

"Leave them on," Paul said to Duncan as he bent to untie his shoes inside. "The place is a bit messy."

Paul's flat was messy, and small. It was one room with low, slanted walls, tiny windows with blinds instead of curtains. The smell of paint thinner and oils was strong and Duncan was pleasantly surprised when a large white cat came running across the room and started to rub up against his legs.

"That's Fish," Paul said. "And her name is Cat," he added, nodding at a single goldfish in a small aquarium on a side table where Paul dropped his house keys.

Duncan found the cat's purring reassuring and he started to relax. The walls were covered with Paul's art and there was a table in the middle of the room with large coffee cans stuffed with paintbrushes, as well as a canvas that Paul was working on. There was an unmade bed against the wall that Duncan tried not to look at.

"Are you okay?" Paul asked.

"Not really," he said.

"What do you mean?" Paul asked, as he sat on the sofa and motioned Duncan to sit next to him.

"I feel like a country hick."

"You don't have to do this. Honestly, no pressure."

Paul walked over to the entranceway closet and took out two umbrellas.

"This is something no good Scotsman ever does without," he said, handing Duncan one of the umbrellas.

"But I want to stay. I'm shy, I guess."

Paul knelt down on the floor in front of Duncan and looked up. They kissed for a minute and Duncan began to relax.

Paul stood, and took his time walking around the room lighting candles. Duncan thought back to his earlier attempt at being "wild." He had taken the bus from Kincardine to Toronto. He and Siobhan had decided to celebrate his graduation from college by having a weekend in the city. We'll stay somewhere in the Church/Wellesley village, Siobhan had announced with an air of worldly confidence. And together they'd Googled a B&B on Dundonald Street. Convincing Skye was a bit of a challenge, but she was proud of his accomplishments and Duncan reminded her that he'd never given her any reason to doubt him in the past — *besides*, he'd told her, *I could have done anything I wanted for the last three years at Western.*

Skye agreed with him, and to seal the deal she gave Siobhan one of her famous looks when she arrived to pick Duncan up.

*Oh Skye, chill*, Siobhan said. *I'll bring him home in one piece.*

It was an easy walk from the bus station on Bay Street and Siobhan and Duncan stopped at a liquor store on the way to buy a bottle of wine.

At the Dundonald Guest House, they unpacked and agreed to meet in Siobhan's room for a drink.

"To freedom." Siobhan tapped her glass against Duncan's.

"To getting laid," Duncan said, embarrassed at how false those words sounded. He was never good at acting like a hotshot.

"You be careful out there tonight," Siobhan said. "Start out at Woody's. I've heard that place is pretty tame."

They walked to Church Street together and Siobhan left him on the steps at Woody's.

"See you at breakfast," Siobhan said, kissing him on the cheek.

Duncan wasn't in the bar very long before he was approached by a guy named Alex offering to buy him a beer. They drank the beer and talked for a few minutes and then Duncan bought a round; and then they returned to the same conversation about their favourite movies. Alex was Greek and invited Duncan to his place on the Danforth. Duncan hesitated, but after a third beer, they flagged a taxi on the street in front of the bar. But the whole thing was too unnerving for Duncan, and he asked the driver to pull over at the Pape subway station.

Over breakfast the next morning, he bragged to Siobhan about how easy it all was, but she saw right through him.

"You didn't go home with anyone, did you?"

"Not really," he said, embarrassed to be caught in a lie.

•

When Paul had lit the last candle, he put on a CD and came back to sit beside Duncan.

"How are you doing?" he asked.

"Good," said Duncan, but he wasn't so sure.

"You're nervous," Paul said. "Let's talk."

"About?"

"Anything," Paul said. "Why don't you tell me about your exhibition at Summerhall?"

"Well," said Duncan, happy to have a distraction. "I was sitting in a coffee shop in Kincardine doodling and thinking about the cover of a *National Enquirer* I had seen earlier that day in a drugstore... you guys get *National Enquirer* over here, don't you?"

"The Brits invented the *National Enquirer*," Paul said, sitting closer to Duncan.

"Well, there was a blurred shot of a semi-naked boy with long, scruffy hair running through a forest; the caption across the front page read *I Was Raised by a Pack of Kind-Hearted Wolves.*"

"Irresistible," Paul said.

"Well, I did one drawing and then another and then another... you know how it goes when you finally find something you can sink your teeth into."

"Uh huh," Paul said, kissing Duncan's hand.

"Well, Wolf Boy gets a mate and he is sexy like the guys in all those vampire movies that are out now...the drawings get pretty hot..."

"I know," said Paul. "I've seen the show. I would have never guessed that the artist was a shy guy like you."

Duncan blushed, but continued. "My life has been a little strange," he said. "And as I kept going, some of that strangeness showed up in the drawings."

"Everyone's life is a little strange," Paul said.

"I don't know about that. Sometimes I wonder if only artists are totally off-the-wall."

"Artists talk about it. They show it in their work so it's visible to others. I'm not sure we are the only strange ones on the planet though."

"Anyhow," said Duncan, squeezing Paul's hand. "One of the drawings that came out that day really shook me up."

"The one with two hot, ripped wolves making out?"

"That's the one. You see, it's kind of a long story," he began, stopping to look at Paul's reaction. "When I was about two, my dad had been drinking and driving and got into a really bad car accident, and then he got all messed up and took off. Apparently he's alive and homeless on the streets of Toronto."

"That's pretty sad," said Paul inching closer, putting his arm around Duncan's shoulder. "Go on…"

As he spoke, Duncan realized that his life story *was* weird.

"Skye was the town eccentric. We created this world together. Crazy art, two-people plays…she would tell me all these animal stories. Even the blanket I used as a kid was supposed to contain mystical powers."

"Do you miss your dad?"

Duncan was taken aback. "I guess," he said. "But screw him… I've lived in the same house and the same town my entire life and he's never tried to find me."

"Maybe he feels bad."

"Bad! His stupidity killed my mother and then he runs off for thirty years. Bad!?"

"Whoa," said Paul, holding Duncan. "Whoa…"

And when Duncan finally stopped shaking from anger, he began to sob. He was aware that he was breaking down in front of a complete stranger, but he didn't care. He sobbed as Paul rocked him in his arms, kissed the top of his head.

"So," said Paul when Duncan stopped crying, "which of your parents had the good looks?"

"My mom," Duncan said, taking a deep breath, putting his hand under Paul's T-shirt.

Paul kissed him, and when Duncan kissed him back, he kissed him with everything he had. No doubt in his mind about who he wanted to be with. No doubt in his mind where he was going to spend the night.

# KINCARDINE, 2011

When Skye died, a dozen white doves did not descend from a gathering of fluffy clouds. There was no stream of heavenly light or singing angels. There wasn't a moment of silence in the forest, and a wolf didn't pause, then howl twice at the waning moon. The tightening in her chest had returned and she curled in a ball, her grey hair partly covering her face; she imagined that she was clutching Rocky close to her. She could smell his coat, warm from the sun. She imagined his cold nose against her wrist. She breathed in deeply and held the breath: *Hold fast*, her father told her the day she and Rory boarded the ship from Leith.

But Duncan ...

# EDINBURGH, 2011

Siobhan took the window, Duncan sat in the middle, and Paul took the aisle seat on the plane — within ten hours of Duncan speaking with Cathy, the three of them were on a flight to Toronto.

Paul knew a travel agent who found them emergency seats on a flight through Amsterdam. He had helped Duncan pack and picked up Siobhan at the front door of the dorm where she was staying.

"This is going to be hard for him," she said, nodding in the direction of the car.

"And you?" he asked.

"Not so hot," she said, as she slid into the back seat behind Duncan.

## AFRICAN BUSH ELEPHANT

| Species | Loxodonta africana |
|---|---|
| Phylum | Chordata |
| Order | Proboscidea |
| Family | Elephantidae |
| Description | The largest living terrestrial animal on the planet. Large head and two enormous, round ears that fan off heat; a muscular trunk used for smelling, drinking, bathing and greeting. |
| Attributes | They don't have the good memory they are credited for, but a good one nonetheless. They are feeling creatures — grieving for the dead with a forest of tears. |

*Life Lesson for Duncan*
Love yourself; love someone else — no rules but that.

# TORONTO, 2011

The day starts out foggy but gradually tree tips become visible as well as the top floors of the downtown Toronto high-rises. Hundreds of people arrive on foot, many ringing bicycle bells as they push them down the sidewalk or across David Pecaut Square. Siobhan, Paul and Duncan find a place to sit on the grass close to Roy Thomson Hall where the service is being held; giant monitors have been set up for the overflow crowd.

All three of them wear orange T-shirts. And although it's a sombre occasion and Duncan is somewhat numb with grief and travel, he is also content to be sitting in the sun on a late summer day. He thinks about Skye's funeral just two days earlier. The entire town seemed to be there. Even the mayor of Kincardine showed up for the service with a story about how Skye saved his dog after it had been hit by a rambunctious teenager on his motorcycle. It didn't take much convincing from Siobhan to get Duncan to attend Layton's funeral. *Skye would have wanted you to go*, she said. *In spirit, she'll be there too.*

"Why the bicycle bells?" Paul asks, as the crowd continues to grow.

"Jack Layton was a bike guy. He rode his to City Hall every day," Siobhan says.

As they speak, the monitor at the back of Pecaut Square lights up, showing the procession through the downtown streets; the bagpipes and the flag-draped coffin passing City Hall as people cheer; Olivia Chow following behind the hearse on foot. Everyone stands as the casket arrives at Roy Thomson Hall; the Toronto Symphony Orchestra plays *Adagio for Strings*.

Paul slips his arm around Duncan's waist; they lower their heads as Olivia Chow speaks: *We're sad*, she says ...*let's look forward.*

His worker, Jo, is there for discharge and she promises the staff at the hospital that she will take Magnus to the men's shelter where he'll stay before making the trip to Kincardine on the bus.

"There's a big funeral today," she tells Magnus as he steps up into the outreach van. "There might be traffic problems, but we'll get there."

Magnus has been sober for almost three weeks and he feels like a different person.

They told him that he had *complications related to acute alcoholism and PTSD.*

*Post-traumatic stress disorder*, Jo explains, looks over at Magnus as he clutches the blue bag in his lap. *In plain English, it means you've been freaked out for a long time.*

"Who died?" Magnus asks her as the van pulls into the traffic on Church Street.

"Jack Layton. And there's going to be a funeral down at your old stomping grounds."

Magnus is hurt by Jo's comment. Not the Jack Layton part; it's the *old stomping grounds* comment that makes him embarrassed.

"I'm never going back there, Jo," he says, digging into his pocket, squeezing Skye's rusty grouse foot pin.

"I'm with you, Mister S," she says. "Let's go."

The staff at Seaton House shelter ask if he has anything that he would like them to hold. *Anything to hold* is code for no alcohol on the premises, and Magnus is proud to say he has nothing to give them. "Except," he asks, handing the blue bag over the counter to the staff. "Do you mind storing this?"

He sits on the side of his cot with his hands in his pockets, rolling the grouse foot over and over in his fingers. As usual, the place is full of men like him: homeless and alone, living day to day. But this time things are different. Magnus is afraid to be among the men who are sometimes volatile and the smell of urine and alcohol makes him feel sick. What is it that Skye wants him to pass on? What is he supposed to tell Duncan about love and rules?

His decision to go for a walk has everything to do with wanting to get some fresh air and nothing to do with sitting at his old spot in front of Roy Thomson Hall, but that's where he is headed. His feet hurt and he has a headache, but he is able to walk straight and people don't cross the street to avoid him. There's a lot of traffic and more people on the sidewalks than usual. And it's getting hot, so he takes off his coat as he walks. When he looks up the street into the sun, he sees a group of mounted police leading a hearse. It's like a mirage at first, the horses prancing sideways and the procession of black cars flickering in the sun. *Your old stomping grounds*, Jo said, and it hurt. But here he is about to settle down by the Walk of Fame. There will be lots of sympathetic people at the funeral who will give him money. His Frisbee is gone, so he looks for an empty coffee cup or something else to put money in. *I still need to live*, he convinces himself as he digs through a garbage bin. *Stinkin' thinkin'* he remembers Jo's voice teasing him about how his cravings will trick him into doing things that will lead to drinking. *You're kidding yourself if you think otherwise.*

"Keep moving." He hears a man's voice.

It has been a long time since he has been able to bring himself to look a police officer in the face, but he does. "Thank you, officer," he says, getting to his feet.

When Stephen Lewis delivers his eulogy the crowd stands and applauds for a long time before gently settling down.

"Wow," says Paul, looking at Duncan.

"Yes," says Siobhan, tearing up.

And, a few minutes later when the first chords of the song are struck, and Lorraine Segato comes onto the stage to sing "Rise Up," everyone stands and the mood picks up again.

Siobhan starts dancing; Paul and Duncan clap their hands.

"This was our anthem in the '80s," Duncan shouts above the music.

"You weren't even born then," Paul laughs.

"I was a baby…but this song has been on the radio for years. We used it for Layton's campaign."

There aren't many places left to sit or stand in the Square anymore and Duncan does his best to hang onto their spot in the grass as the crowd continues to grow and new people push their way in.

…*Rise up, rise up. Rise in the city of power* …

Although there is a spirit of celebration mixed with grief, there is also a sense of unease among the crowd. The great *ah ha* of Layton's spirit; the perfect note to release their grief.

For Duncan, it was the great *ah ha* of knowing Skye was somehow present.

Not everyone sits down when the song ends and the next speaker takes the stage; someone squeezes through the crowd — an old man; a scruffy, short guy blocks their view.

"Excuse me," Siobhan shouts at his back.

"Hello?" says Duncan. "Sir, you're blocking our view."

Magnus drops his coat on the ground and as he bends to pick it up he notices that the young man behind him who has asked him to move is sitting arm-in-arm with another man. He starts to move along, but an insistent woman's voice rises above the crowd: *Please sit down!*

Magnus drops his coat on the grass and sits on it. He wants a drink. More than anything else in the world, he wishes he could dig inside his coat pocket and find a bottle of Lauder's. He wishes he were back in the darkness of the Silos, away from all these people.

"Who was that?" asks Paul, looking over the crowd to find the woman who had called out to the old man. "I'm sure she said your name."

"I think I know," says Duncan, shivering as the sun slides behind a cloud.

Duncan stretches back in the grass. As Stephen Page sings *Hallelujah*, his thoughts wander back to Scotland and those last hours rushing to pick up Siobhan at the dorm, then driving back to the Roxburghe Hotel to get his things.

"I'm coming with you," Paul insisted as they sat, side by side, on the bed at the Roxburghe. And although Duncan was stunned by the words, he didn't question Paul's decision.

"I'm coming with you. I'll stay in a hotel if you want."

"Oh no, you won't," Duncan said. "I mean, that would be great…and no, you don't…you know what I mean," he added, pulling Paul close: "No more hotels for either of us."

Skye had been old for as long as he could remember, and Duncan assumed that once she reached her late eighties her time would come sooner rather than later; but the impact was profound. He couldn't find the door card for his hotel room. He couldn't find his wallet with his credit cards and passport.

"Be calm," Paul said. "Be logical about where you would have put them."

Duncan sat on the side of the bed with his head in his hands, thinking. Finally, he remembered that he had left his passport at the front desk when he checked in, and his door card and wallet were in his backpack.

"This is BIG," Siobhan had said when she spoke to Duncan on his cellphone. "He's coming with us to Toronto and then the two of you are moving to Scotland?"

Duncan looks around at the people who have gathered; the entire Square seems to radiate orange and gold, and there is a subtle hint of fall in the August breeze. Duncan is drawn to the old man in front of him — probably homeless; maybe crazy? The old guy fidgets, and Duncan thinks about Layton's advocacy for the homeless. He thinks about his father. There aren't many homeless people in Kincardine; the homeless go to the city to hide — it's easier, Duncan imagines, among thousands of indifferent strangers.

He digs deep inside himself, wondering why the tears won't come. His childhood was strange but happy. He remembers how everything seemed ecstatic — toads and rabbits, the birds and butterflies moving through beams of sunlight. The crazy stories about animals and ancient castles that Skye would tell him to keep him entertained. There are few carefree days like that anymore. He worries about his students the same way he'd always worried about Skye. He looks over at Siobhan digging through her backpack for a joint — he worries about her too. He questions his talent as an artist and he has wondered about whether it's his destiny to be alone. He knows he's very private and too quirky for most. He allows himself to float up over the crowd of people. He floats across the video monitor and he circles above the thousands of people in the Square. It's hard to accept that Skye is dead. He's certain that she's here. On the ground, he looks up again and is drawn to the old man in front of him who is trying to stand, only he can't seem to get to his feet.

*Move*, shouts the woman's voice again, only this time Duncan knows the voice is meant for him.

"Are you all right?" Duncan asks, holding the old man's arm and helping him to his feet.

*Perfect*, he hears the woman's voice say. He turns and looks for her among the crowd, but can't attach the voice to a body. He listens again. *Open your eyes, Duncan*, the voice says, only now he knows that she's inside his head. But he can't, not this very second — he knows what the nudge is about; he understands why Skye's here, but can't bring himself to look.

"Let me help," says Paul, taking the old man's other arm. Siobhan is next to him carrying the backpacks. "Let's go," she says, and the four of them push their way through the crowd of mourners sitting and standing in the square.

It's always the same dream — Duncan is walking in a forest; it could be Africa, it could be Algonquin Park — sometimes the trees look deciduous, sometimes they're tropical. He comes to a clearing where there's a herd of elephants. He is astonished by their size and excited by the encounter. He is young, perhaps six or seven years old. In the dream, he walks toward the baby elephant. The mother elephant flaps her ears and he can feel her power. He stops. She stomps and trumpets. A warning he ignores.

He always woke with the bull elephant's foot on his throat; always gasping for air. And sometimes he would turn on his bedside lamp and look at the picture of Moira and Magnus that Skye had placed there. Once, when he was small, Skye told him, he crumpled the picture and put it in his mouth.

Magnus recognizes his son from the picture that Skye had given him the day that she came to the silo. "I'm fine," he says, trying to put on his coat. He is happy to be away from the crowds of people. The King streetcar clangs as it goes by slowly; it has a black bow attached to its front bumper. As Magnus struggles to put his arm into the sleeve the grouse foot pin falls from the pocket and Duncan bends to pick it up.

"This looks just like Skye's pin," he says to Siobhan, holding it up to the sunlight so she can see the purple stone and silver detail that made it unique. "Remember? She always wore one just like this on her."

"That *is* her pin," says Magnus, sheltering his eyes from the sun with his sleeve. "And it's yours now," he adds, looking at the pin in his son's hand. "It comes with a message from Skye."

Magnus struggles to remember the message.

"Something about love and no rules," he says, feeling stupid.

Duncan looks at the weather-beaten man with grey hair wearing a torn winter coat on a hot August day. He can't decide if he should hug or punch him. He isn't sure what to say, so he says nothing.

"Who is this?" asks Paul, looking at Duncan, then to Siobhan.

"No one," says Duncan, finally able to speak, squeezing the brooch in his hand as he turns away.

"Wait!" Siobhan says, as Magnus walks away. "Do you live far? Can we help you?"

"Down by the lake," Magnus says. "I don't need help. Thank you."

It has been a long time since Magnus had a real conversation with people. When he used to sit on the Walk of Fame, he'd hold up a piece of cardboard: *Spare Change?* Occasionally someone would stop and talk to him — usually someone from a church. They would ask how he got on the street or if he'd found Jesus. Some would get more personal — have you ever been married? Or, did you *ever* have a job? Magnus would look away from these people and pretend he didn't speak English. He would hold up his sign or stick out his hand, and they would almost always walk away. Except Jo. When the Outreach van pulled up she would step out of the sliding doors with a blanket and a coffee in her hand — *Double double*, she would say. Then she would ask if he wanted *tuna or ham and cheese?*

Magnus would always say *thank you* to Jo, and occasionally, if he wasn't too drunk, he'd even talk a little.

*I got kicked in the head*, he told her once, showing Jo the scar on the top of his head. *In a bar fight when I was young.*

And when she put her hand over the scar, with no hesitation or putting on rubber gloves first the way the ambulance drivers always did, he hung his head and cried. *I'm so screwed up*, he told her.

Jo left her hand on his head and started to cry herself: *No you're not, Mister S*, she said. *You're hurt. There's a difference, you know.*

※

The abandoned silo is at the narrow mouth of the port; a teetering, grey monolith ready to tumble into the lake. Magnus keeps it in sight as he walks down the street as fast as he can. He kept his promise to

Skye and passed on the brooch and her message; now he can go back to his life. He rips off the two-by-four that has been nailed across the door and steps into the silo, the comfort of the dark. He works his way over to the mattress covered with the torn-apart bears and as he reaches into his coat for the bottle of Lauder's he hesitates.

# KINCARDINE, 2011

The spirit of a hundred thousand dead animals is the wind howling like a wolf, thrashing like a herd of elephants through the house. Strong and determined, it rushes up the stairs from the basement and scatters the drawings that Duncan is working on onto the kitchen floor. Duncan turns and pauses, looks down into the dark, before picking up the drawings and closing the door. He's alone in the house and enjoying the solitude while Paul and Siobhan fetch the last of Siobhan's belongings from the Royal Apartments. He sits and slides open the drawer at the end of the table where Skye had always sat. There had been an unspoken rule that the drawer was hers alone; a private place where she kept her sketchbook and pencils. The wind blows and the basement door opens again; for a brief second Duncan is alarmed.

*Skye,* he sighs. *I'm here.*

He pulls out the journal and sets it on the table — it's well worn, heavier than it looks. He opens the front page and sees large, scrolling letters: *Life Lessons for Duncan.* His heart pounds and his throat tightens — it still seems impossible that Skye is gone. As he turns to the first page of the book, he sees a playful drawing of a squirrel.

*Squirrel: Sciurus carolinensis*

He chuckles to himself, remembers Skye's disdain for squirrels — how angry she got when he brought one into the house. *Rodent!* she said. He remembers how disturbed she was when he'd told her about the squirrel who visited him in bed when he was a kid. He continues to leaf through the pages. The illustrations are simple and beautiful; the care that Skye put into the book is evident in the fine script and detailed drawings.

*Crow: Corvus brachyrhynchos*
*Dog: Canis lupus familiaris*

Duncan reads about the grouse foot brooch and how Skye had passed it on to Magnus.

*Take what he gives you for what it is, a worthless kilt pin; but look beyond the dirt of the man who puts it in your hand...open your mind and heart, especially when it's your father standing in front of you.*

Duncan sets the journal down on the table and leans back in the chair. The wind has calmed down and the sun is coming through the kitchen window. She went to him, he thinks. Skye wandered the streets of Toronto looking for Magnus. Where would she go? How would she know where to look? He wonders if his response to meeting his father would have been different if he had read through this book first.

Duncan picks up the journal again and opens it to the end. There's a full-page drawing of an elephant. Like the one from his dreams, it's a male with enormous ears and tusks; but unlike the elephant of his dreams, this one is calm and, as he looks closely, Duncan can see what looks like a tear rolling down its rough, grey skin:

*African Bush Elephant: Loxodonta africana*
*Life Lesson for Duncan: Love yourself. Love someone else — no rules but that.*

Skye would have liked Paul. She would have appreciated his free spirit and loved his strong Scottish accent.

*So pleased to meet you, Skye Rayburn,* he would have said, rolling the big R in Rayburn with just the right intonation. He would have charmed her, possibly kissed her on the cheek or handed her flowers. *Duncan tells me that you are the best veterinarian this side of the ocean,* he would have said, standing at the front door of their house.

Skye would have been proud. She would have been glad that Duncan fell for someone as confident as Paul. She would have been awkward at first, but pleased, in the end, to invite him into the house. *Oh, dear man,* he imagines her saying. *Please sit yourself down. You must be exhausted from the journey. I came over on a boat...*she would have told him. *The water was rough and some of us were ill.* And then she may have gone silent for a few seconds, the way she always did when she got to the part about being sick on the boat.

•

Duncan flips to the back of the journal and reads: *Some people shouldn't own animals...and some people shouldn't have children.*

The shock of that sentence is disturbing to him; yet, he had never known Skye to pull punches, why would she do it here?

*I've never told you how impossible it became after that experience with the puppy mill for me to see human beings the same...I felt helpless to do anything about the children. And remained that way for a long time, until finally, out of the blue one day, I started to understand your father...perhaps his desertion was an act of compassion? Perhaps he believed that you would have been better off without him?*

When he was young and had imagined the reunion, he always saw himself more accepting of his father — sometimes the fantasy had them hugging one another and expressing an instant bond, and sometimes it was more subdued. Across the various scenarios, Duncan had always pictured his father uttering his first words. *I'm sorry.* Over and over.

But, instead, his father walked in one direction and he walked in the other. There were no apologies or hugs. There was no bond or affection.

*Of course I'm your father,* he had hoped his father would say. *I'm sorry, and I'm back this time for good.*

•

*I couldn't bring myself to tell you,* Skye wrote. *I had my reasons at the time.*

*Siobhan is your sister,* she continued. *Once you've met your father, you'll see what I'm saying. She looks like him. She has his troubled disposition and his shining eyes.*

How could she? How could she not tell me something so important?

*As I write this note the two of you are on your way to Edinburgh together. How strange and wonderfully insistent life is — the two of you side by side.*

*And your mother. Dear Duncan, your mother wasn't perfect — please don't blame your father. Your mother needed to prove herself, to me, I'm the one to blame for her recklessness.*

Duncan opens the drawer at the end of the table and slides the journal back inside. His heart is racing and he's happy and sad in equal measures. He reaches into his backpack and feels around for his cellphone. He dials Siobhan's number and hears her voice differently now — the voice is the voice of his sister, the high-pitched sound of a sibling.

"Siobhan," he says. "Get over here!"

*MANKIND*

| Species | Homo sapiens |
|---|---|
| Phylum | Chordata |
| Order | Primate |
| Family | Hominidae |
| Description | Originally from Africa, body size is largely determined by genetics: the average human female weighs between 120 and 140 pounds; males, between 168 and 183. Pair-bonding and sexuality are important aspects of social structure and serve important survival functions. Love is as common as hate, envy, or grief — it is often inter-species, and not fully understood. |
| Attributes | Their larger brain gives them status among the animal kingdom; their capacity for harm is presently dwarfed by their capacity for good. |

*Life Lesson for Duncan*

After eight weeks of gestation the embryo becomes a fetus.

When you were born, the crows cawed, the sparrows sang and the trees swayed under the heat of late August sun — be what you were meant to be, dear boy...fly far...

# KINCARDINE, 2011

Although two drawings accompany the journal entry, they only take up a few inches on the bottom of the page. Duncan leans in close to see the details. The woman with blue eyes and gentle expression is, without a doubt, Skye. She is young and beautiful. There are no wrinkles on her face, no crow's feet at the corners of her eyes or distress in her smile. Above her chest, she cradles what looks like a live, beating heart; it isn't sad or morbid though — it's as if self-compassion revealed itself to Skye and came to rest in the palm of her hand. There are women, men, children and animals, all surrounded by halos of light. By virtue of swirling lines and overlapping colours, they all appear to be extensions of Skye. The second drawing is of a bird opening its mouth to receive a worm. It's a glowing worm and the worm seems to be emerging from a shell. The bird is silhouetted by the moon and the same moon is reflected in its eye: she has written *Bir Bir* beneath her drawing.

•

Duncan sat at the kitchen table and opened the box with Paul looking over his shoulder.

"Holy…" Paul said, "they're just like the miniature Burke caskets from Arthur's Seat!"

"Who is Burke?" Duncan asked.

"Burke and Hare were serial killers who sold their victim's bodies to the medical schools in Edinburgh to be experimented on."

"Yikes," said Duncan. "Why would Skye leave me something like this?"

•

A few days later, just as Duncan turns on the burner to boil water for tea, the doorbell rings. For a sun-blinded second he doesn't recognize the man standing at the door with a blue bag his hand. His father, in a clean white shirt, has shaved off his beard and cut his hair. His smile is tentative but his eyes are clear and focussed.

"Skye had a bit of an obsession with what she called the *three Big M's*," Magnus says, handing Duncan a blue bag. "*Money, Manners and Marriage,* she'd say."

Duncan doesn't take the bag but his deep sense of good manners insists that he invite the man into the house. "I'm making tea," he says.

"This place hasn't changed a bit," Magnus says, as he follows his son along the dark hallway toward the kitchen. "Same squeaky hardwood. Same old pictures on the wall."

Magnus stops to point up at a framed black-and-white photograph of the Roxburghe Hotel. "That's where Skye stayed on her wedding night. She must have told us that story a million times. Moira," Magnus says, looking down at the floor. "Your mother did her best to seem interested in her mother's story."

"I was just there," Duncan says, still debating whether to have a conversation with this man or not. "At the Roxburghe, in Edinburgh."

"I'm no stranger, you know," Magnus says, stopping in the kitchen doorway. He hands Duncan the blue bag again. "I'm your father," he adds. "You don't have to be shy with me."

Duncan takes the dirty bag from Magnus. He feels the weight of what's inside and the weight of Magnus's words and begins to shake.

"You ARE a fucking stranger," he yells. "I don't have a fucking clue who you are. I've lived my entire life without you and now you want to pretend we're father and son."

When Duncan throws the bag against the wall above the stove, clusters of green twenties and pink fifties hit the stove top, along with patches of blue five dollar bills, and the occasional fanned-out stack of mauve tens. There are photographs and the tattered gold blanket as well — all this, just as the kettle whistles loud and annoying and shrill.

"Holy shit," Magnus says, running toward the stove.

The two of them grab the money. As one of the pictures catches fire, Duncan smothers the flame with the gold blanket.

"This old, gold blanket," he asks, looking at Magnus. "How?"

"Skye," Magnus says, picking up the partly burned photograph, "This is you, me and your mother."

"Let me see," Duncan says, reaching for the scorched picture of him with his mother and father. His mother looking exhausted and sad, his father's eyes half closed, ready to pass out or cry.

"How?" he asks, hesitating for a few seconds before digging into the second part of his question. "How could you not come back here for me?"

"Because the hole just got deeper. Deeper and deeper and I couldn't dig out. But now I'm out and at the Royal Apartments again after all this time."

"How 'bout the hole you left me in? How do you think it felt growing up here with no parents and Skye doing everything by herself?"

"Looks pretty good to me," Magnus says, looking around the bright yellow kitchen. "Better than the hole I dug out of."

"Your choice," says Duncan, picking more bills off the stove. "You had a choice. I didn't."

"I didn't have a choice, son," Magnus says with a deep sadness and sincerity that cuts across nearly three decades. "Your mother was too drunk to drive that night. It was my birthday but I stopped drinking so I could drive."

*That night.* The night that no one talks about.

Duncan stands perfectly still. He can't step forward. He can't step back and he can't sit down. When his father extends his arms, Duncan leans into the hug and begins to cry. Not sad tears. Not grief. Not loss or death. Relief.

"Money, manners and marriage," Duncan says, when he finally looks up at his father. "Skye said it was all very simple."

"Easier said than done," says Magnus.

"Tell me about it."

# EDINBURGH, 2012

A twelve-year-old British girl named Tia, who had been missing for a week, has been found dead in her grandmother's apartment. The grandmother's boyfriend is accused of murder.

The United States has won one hundred and four medals; the United Kingdom, sixty-five; and Canada, eighteen. Nicola Adams won the Olympic gold medal in flyweight women's boxing.

Summerhall has become the largest venue for the Edinburgh Fringe Festival.

•

Paul and Duncan stand at the base of Arthur's Seat looking up to the top of the mountain. Duncan holds a small bag; inside is the blue box with the miniature caskets and Rocky's collar.

*Find a grassy patch among the rocks on Arthur's Seat and bury this blue box with the tiny caskets,* Skye had written in the journal. *I will not explain,* she wrote. *I am at peace with the past. I know I'm being sentimental,* she continued, *but I wanted to send something of Rocky home as well. Please scatter his ashes with the others.*

Duncan's decision to move to Edinburgh was easy once he let down his guard. How could he possibly say no to Paul with his soaring spirit and passion? He couldn't say no to the two of them together — side by side, sweating, laughing, climbing the winding path.

"Let's go," Duncan says, squeezing Paul's hand.

"Yes," Paul says. "Up this craggy old hill before it gets dark."

# EDINBURGH, 1945

The day before they left for Canada from the harbour at Leith, Skye asked Rory to take her to Arthur's Seat one last time. She said her farewells to Anne on the steps in front of the Royal Dick and then she and Rory walked in the sunshine along Holyrood Park Road to the base of the mountain. She hadn't regained her strength and the walk was slow and difficult. Each step across the uneven base of the mountain seemed more laboured than the one that preceded it. As they came to the end of their climb, Skye stopped for a moment to look up at the sun. She inhaled and carefully stepped along the rock path. At the top, she sat down next to Rory and looked, one last time, out over the rooftops of the city. The Firth of Forth stretching in from the North Sea on her right, and Edinburgh Castle silhouetted against the setting sun of an evening sky in front of her; something caught her attention over the Royal Dick buildings. It wasn't smoke, and there wasn't even the smallest of rain clouds in the sky, but Skye swore she could see something rising over the rooftops of the Royal Dick buildings. Like small grey clusters of sheep's wool or billowing streams of fireplace smoke, they arrived in pairs — two camels and two elephants, followed by a pair of small dogs and parallel strings of smoke like mating snakes. Rory sat beside her, respectful of her silent farewell, but had he known what she was witnessing he may have decided to leave her in Scotland. Strange and somehow natural, it was as if all of those animals that had their final hours in the Dissection Room theatre were rising at once through the sky. Skye was pleased to see them — the laboratory rats and the worked-to-death plough horses; the sparrows and great gold eagle. But as the final two figures took shape over the rooftop, Skye held her breath — the swollen little legs and the unformed arms, two tiny infants, a boy and a girl, lost among the smoke of the animal herd. What's wrong? Rory pleaded, but Skye couldn't answer. She wanted to throw herself off the mountain, fly through the sky to the apparition — *I'll be back,* she promised. Then the pair of them stood and walked back down the mountain.

"We can do this," Rory said, stopping in front of her on the path.

"Yes," she said, looking across the water to Canada. "Taller mountains, deeper valleys, the same rough sea."

# ACKNOWLEDGMENTS

When Robert McDowell welcomed me onto the stage of what was once the dissection room of Edinburgh's Royal Dick Veterinarian College by announcing that I was about to read in a room filled with "the spirits of a hundred thousand dead animals," I knew immediately that his words contained the essence of a novel — thank you, Robert, for that weird and wonderful introduction.

Marnie Woodrow, thank you for coaching me through early stages of scene building and character development; your encouragement and prompts were crucial to coaxing these characters from the ether of my imagination into bright-light real-life existence. Bethany Gibson, Vivette Kady, and Michael Redhill: thank you for your edits, insights and challenges, and for helping me to disentangle the years and voices woven through these pages. And to Eddy Yanofsky, Laura Lush, Sue Collins, Barry Dempster, Maureen Scott-Harris, Kelley Aitken, David Rayfield, Ed Koetanen — I am filled with gratitude for your friendship, your commitment to art, and the wisdom and integrity you bring to the world.

Maureen Hynes and Elizabeth Ukrainetz — thank you for your close readings and insights. And to Don Smith, for your love and the way you believed in the book from day one, for the way you inspired and encouraged me as I wrote, and for introducing me to Kincardine: thank you. I send a heartfelt wave of gratitude to the very fine people of Kincardine where much of the book was written. Especially, to Allison Hooper, the veterinarian extraordinaire, who taught me about cows that swallow apples and the horror of small-town puppy mills. Cindy, Bill, Debbie, Jim, Laurie, Michael, Gail, Lisa, Lynn, Shirley, Vern, Margo, Gloria — Kincardine is a fine, fine place to live because you are there.

I want to thank my present-day family and remember my grandparents and great-grandparents who came from "across the pond." Thank you to my siblings Siovhon, Bill, Steve, Mike, Ron and Earl and to my parents. And, dear Joyce, thank you for encouraging and inspiring me all these years and for the real life-force you gave to fictional Skye.

Finally, I would like to thank Karen Haughian and the dedicated and talented team at Signature Editions for publishing the book and bringing *Spirit* to the world.

## ABOUT THE AUTHOR

Award-winning author Jim Nason has published five poetry collections, two previous novels, as well as a short-story collection. His stories, essays and poems have been published in journals and anthologies across Canada and the U. S., including *Best Canadian Poetry in English*, 2008, 2010 and 2014, and he has been a finalist for the CBC Literary Award in both fiction and poetry categories.

Jim holds degrees from McGill, Ryerson and York Universities and is the owner/publisher of Tightrope Books, Toronto. He is the founder and organizer of Canada's annual human rights poetry event, Meet Me in the Middle: Writers on Rights.

Jim is a frequent participant on fiction and poetry panels. *Spirit of a Hundred Thousand Dead Animals* was inspired at the Edinburgh International Fringe Festival where Jim was a participant on a panel about sexuality in Canadian poetry: The Frigid North.

Eco-Audit
*Printing this book using Rolland Enviro 100 Book*
*instead of virgin fibres paper saved the following resources:*

| Trees | Solid Waste | Water | Air Emissions |
|:-----:|:-----------:|:-------:|:-------------:|
| 3 | 151 kg | 12,292 L | 495 kg |